BETRAYAL AT THE B&B

A WHODUNIT PET COZY MYSTERY SERIES BOOK 2

MEL MCCOY

CHAPTER 1

Sarah Shores heard the waves crashing off to her left as she walked south along the board-walk. Out for a walk with Winston and Rugby, she noticed that the beachside shops were open and bursting at the seams with tourists. The season was in full swing, and Sarah was excited to spend the rest of the summer in Cascade Cove, Florida.

"Easy, Rugby," she said, feeling the yellow lab pull slightly. To their right, coming toward them, a pair of Yorkshire terriers led an elderly couple along in the opposite direction.

The Yorkies yapped at Rugby, who pulled the lead more to say hello.

Sarah said hello to the couple, who seemed eager for their dogs to socialize. Winston, the corgi Sarah had rescued, pulled as well, joining Rugby in greeting the two miniature dogs.

Rugby's tail was going in overdrive as he sniffed at his new friends. His shadow eclipsed the two dogs, whose combined weight was only a fraction of the yellow lab's eighty pounds. Even Winston, who was nearly thirty pounds, outweighed their combined weight two-to-one.

"What're their names?" Sarah asked.

The woman smiled. "Penny and Jenny."

"You can tell who named them," the man said with a smirk.

Sarah laughed. "This is Rugby and Winston."

"We used to have a lab before we got these two runts," the old man said, bending down to pet Rugby and Winston.

"Oh, Carl," the woman said, swatting at him.

"Dolores likes small dogs."

Sarah peered down at the two Yorkies. "They are adorable."

"Thank you," Dolores said.

Sarah chatted with the couple for a few minutes while the dogs played, and then they said their goodbyes.

"Enjoy the rest of your day," Carl said, and he and his wife waved to Sarah and her dogs as they walked away.

"You too."

Sarah took a deep breath. The wind was warm, and the air was filled with the smell of saltwater, mixed with soft pretzels, cotton candy, and baked goods.

Up ahead, she spotted the Ferris wheel at the small amusement park, which was located at the southern end of the boardwalk. She smiled at the sight—it would be active later that evening, but now it stood motionless, teasing any passersby who might've been itching for a ride. The view from the top was breathtaking, she remembered, and she couldn't wait to ride the Ferris wheel again soon.

Though she'd been in Cascade Cove for two weeks—visiting her Grandpa and Grandma, along with her cousin, Emma—Sarah hadn't had a chance to ride the Ferris wheel.

Too many other things had gotten in the way...

Her mind drifted to the mysterious death of John Jacobs, a local landowner.

Sarah shook her head, ridding those thoughts from her mind. With that debacle behind the Cove, everything was back to normal, or so she hoped. Though Adam Dunkin told her a body had been found at The Beachside B&B, she didn't yet know the details.

Looking around, it didn't seem as if the town's occupants or tourists had caught wind of it.

The gossip mill wasn't churning, and Sarah was grateful.

"It'll get figured out," she muttered, guiding her dogs along. "Nothing can stop this busy season."

She walked her dogs down to the end of the boardwalk, the Ferris wheel now towering over her.

She turned around and made her way back toward her grandpa's boutique. Once there, she went into Larry's Pawfect Boutique through the boardwalk-side entrance. Inside, she heard familiar voices.

"...and then the man did a belly-flop into the pool," Grandma was saying.

"Oh yeah?" came Adam's voice.

"We had to fish that sucker out of the pool—the belly-flop must've been by mistake, I suppose."

"*You* had to fish him out?"

"Well, not me...that's not what I do on those cruise ships. But one of the other staff members had to. The fellow was drunk as a sailor, if you can believe it."

Sarah let the dogs off their leashes, and they lunged toward Grandma and Adam.

"Oh look, Adam," Grandma said, "Sarah's back already."

Sarah strode up to her Grandma, giving her a big hug. "Hopefully they'll be conked out the rest of the morning."

Grandma chuckled. "If not, they'll drive your grandpa mad."

Ending their embrace, Sarah looked over to the counter and saw Emma sitting on a stool, typing furiously on her laptop.

"Hey, Em," Sarah said.

Emma said something that resembled, "Hey," but didn't look up from her computer, nor did her typing speed slow in the least.

Sarah turned to Adam. "Aren't you on duty now?"

"He is," Grandma said, before Adam could get a word in, "but he's taking time out of his busy day to visit me, since he's such a sweetheart."

Adam's cheeks flushed slightly, and Sarah could tell that he was genuinely glad to hear that Grandma Shores still held him in high regard.

"Oh, Mrs. Shores," Adam said, waving dismissively.

Grandma wrapped her arms around him and squeezed hard, the same way she used to back when he was the boy who used to hang around Sarah and Emma all summer. When he would help them cause trouble around the Cove. Now, as a police officer in Cascade Cove, he was the one setting the troublemakers straight.

"So, Adam," Grandma said, smoothing out her white blouse. "Tell us, what's going on with that body they found at The Beachside B&B?"

Sarah's eyes went wide and she could see Emma perk up from her computer. Her cousin could never pass up information about a body found or a mystery. But Sarah couldn't believe how blunt her grandmother was being. She could now see where her cousin got it from. "Grandma!"

Grandma looked at Sarah. "What?"

"It's okay," Adam said. He turned to Grandma. "I can tell you this much: We found a body and it happened the other night at Cecil's bed and breakfast."

"That's it?" Grandma waved her hand at Adam.

Adam pulled out his notepad from his pocket and flipped it open to a random page, making a show of it.

"The victim is male," he said, then flipped the notebook closed again and put it back in his pocket.

Grandma put her hands on her hips, waiting. "And?"

Adam chuckled. "Mrs. Shores, you know I can't tell you much more than that."

"Bah." Grandma waved her hand at Adam again. "You're no fun."

Emma let out a huff and slid from her stool. "You guys are boring me. I'm going to go upstairs to grab a chocolate chip cookie." She looked at Adam. "I made them last night. You want one?"

It was known around Cascade Cove that Emma didn't share the same talent in the kitchen as her grandma or grandpa. Sarah could see the look of muted trepidation on Adam's face, which matched Grandma's deer-in-the-headlights gaze.

"Uh, no thanks," Adam said. "I've got to get going soon. But thanks."

"Anyone else?"

Sarah and Grandma looked at each other, hoping the other would take one for the team, but they both said "no" in unison.

Grandma added, "Don't want to spoil my dinner, dear."

Nice save, Sarah thought to herself.

"Suit yourself," Emma said, sauntering to the door that led to the upstairs apartment.

Once Emma was surely out of earshot, Sarah asked Grandma, "No cookies for you?"

Grandma shook her head. "That girl needs to learn how to read a recipe."

Sarah and Adam laughed.

Grandma, not paying any mind to them, stepped over to the counter where Emma had sat and ran a finger along the top. She furrowed her brow and wiped her fingers together quickly, to get any dust off. "You know, Cecil and Larry go way back," she said to nobody in particular.

"Oh yeah?" Adam asked.

"Yeah, they used to go bowling together every Friday night. They had a bowling team. What was their name... oh yeah, the Rock Lobsters."

Adam chuckled.

"What?"

"Nothing. So, do they still have the team?"

"No."

"Why not?"

"No reason. Just that Cecil started running a bed and breakfast, and with Larry having the pet boutique...You know how it goes. Just didn't leave much time for them."

"That's too bad," Sarah said.

Grandma nodded. "That's just how life is. People drift in and out of our lives."

"Well," Adam said, "I hate to cut this short, but I really do have to get back to the station."

"See you, sweetheart," Grandma said, giving Adam one final hug before he hurried out the front of the store, back to where his police cruiser was likely parked on the main strip.

Grandma grabbed a rag from under the counter and ran it along the top of the counter.

Sarah said, "I didn't know Grandpa was on a bowling team."

"Who's in charge of dusting this place?"

"I mean, it makes sense…I can see him right at home at a bowling alley, with his Hawaiian shirt and all."

Grandma looked at the rag and grimaced. "Well, it was a while ago. I think you were in college at the time."

Before Sarah could reply, she heard pounding footsteps above them, and yelling. Something was going on upstairs.

Sarah whipped her head toward the front of the store, in time to see Emma rushing into the boutique, frantic.

"What's wrong?" Sarah asked.

"There's a fire in the kitchen!"

Sarah's eyes went wide, and she glanced at her grandma, who also wore a look of disbelief.

"A fire?"

CHAPTER 2

Sarah raced along with Emma as they made their way to the upstairs apartment. She opened the door and rushed in. Smoke hung in the air, and the *whoosh* of a fire extinguisher broke the silence.

Grandma came up beside Sarah as she stood staring at her grandpa, Larry. She placed both hands on her hips and shook her head. "Lawrence, it's like the Quiche Quandary all over again."

Though Larry was a wonderful cook, Sarah remembered that he had a knack for setting kitchen fires, which Grandma liked to bust him on every chance she got.

"Grandpa, are you all right?" Sarah asked.

Larry waved his hand to get rid of the remaining smoke, coaxing it toward the open window by the kitchen sink, coughing. "I put out the fire. Nothing to see here."

Emma crossed her arms. "I guess we're eating out again." She was leaning up against the wall, watching the entire scene unfold.

"Yeah," Larry said. "Looks that way. Any idea where you want to go?"

Emma scratched her chin. "Hmm, maybe the Banana Hammock again."

"Craving the Cascade Burger?" Larry asked.

"Of course."

Sarah's stomach rumbled. "Maybe I'll try that this time. Either that, or the BBQ Burger Adam always gets."

"Okay, let's get things cleaned up," Grandma said. "Lawrence, call and make a reservation for the four of us."

"You got it," Larry said. He roamed toward the master bedroom to retrieve his cell phone.

Grandma started to clean up the mess in the kitchen, and Sarah joined her, making quick work of it, while Emma hurried down to the boutique to ensure there weren't any customers waiting.

A short while later, Emma came back up to the apartment with Rugby, Winston, and Misty in tow.

Misty rushed toward the room that Sarah and Emma shared. She would likely retreat to her spot under the bed, apparently in no mood to play with Rugby and Winston.

The two dogs rushed toward their food bowls, ensuring their dinner would be served.

"I'll take care of them," Sarah said, and she went to feed the dogs.

Suddenly, Misty rushed out from the bedroom and swept past Sarah's legs.

"Want me to feed her too, Em?"

"I'll do it." Emma strode over to the kitchen and, in less than two minutes, both dogs were chowing down, though Misty just picked at her food before she raced off toward the bedroom again.

Sarah's gaze followed the fleeing feline. "Finicky."

Emma gave a quick nod.

"All right, everyone," Larry said, smiling. "Time to get going. Is the shop all closed up, Emma?"

"Yeah, Grandpa. We're golden."

Downstairs, they exited the building out the front of the shop, and Larry double-checked the door to ensure it was locked. He was more careful ensuring the shop was locked up tight, especially during the busy season—and in light of what happened the first week Sarah was in town.

They strode along the main strip, and before long, Sarah spotted the front of the Banana Hammock Bar and Grill. Inside, they were greeted by an unfamiliar face. Sarah wondered where Kacey was, but before she could ask, the hostess waved for them to follow her, and she led them to a table near the window in the corner.

"Thanks, dear," Grandma said.

"You're welcome," the hostess said, passing out menus. "Your waitress will be with you shortly."

The hostess fluttered away, and Sarah scanned the restaurant. Most of the tables were filled up already, though there were a few that were empty. "Good thing we made a reservation," Sarah said, opening her menu. "This place will be filled up soon."

Larry peered out over the top of his menu. "I wouldn't expect any different. Their food is incredible, and they deserve the business."

Grandma adjusted her glasses and squinted. "You'd think they'd have the text bigger on these things."

Reaching into his pocket, Larry pulled something out and handed the object to his wife. "Here."

"A magnifying glass?" she said, looking at Larry like he'd grown an extra head.

Emma nudged Sarah. "This is the stuff you miss out on. Sure you don't want to stay longer than the rest of the summer?"

Sarah had originally been supposed to only be staying with her cousin and grandparents for two weeks, but after the Jacobs murder, she had decided that she'd stay the summer. And why not? She was a teacher in an inner-city school in New York, and she'd have the bulk of the summer off. Of course, that is until a few weeks before school started, and she would need to get back for in-service days to prep for the new school year. Though, the job was definitely wearing on her. She loved teaching and helping kids, but the politics in the school system was more than she could bear and caused the majority of her stress. More than that, she'd been feeling quite lonely by herself in New York and this was becoming more evident to her now while visiting her family in Florida. Emma was right. These were the things she was missing out on.

Before Sarah could reply to her cousin, she saw a familiar face approaching them. The woman wore her brown hair in a ponytail that bobbed as she strode toward them. The corners of her mouth ticked up when she saw Sarah.

Sarah smiled back. "Kacey!"

"Hey, Sarah," Kacey said, pulling a pen from the breast pocket on her green shirt, which bore the Banana Hammock logo. When she glanced up, she spotted Grandma and her smile shone brighter. "Hi, Grandma Ruth! I didn't know you were back already."

Grandma smiled back. "Yes, dear, I cut the trip short,

BETRAYAL AT THE B&B

so I could spend some time with Sarah before she returned to New York, though I hadn't realized she was staying all summer." Grandma reached over the table and patted Sarah's hand, beaming with pride. She trained her eyes on Kacey and asked, "How are you, dear?"

"Oh, you know," Kacey said. "Living the dream."

Grandma chuckled. "How's your father?"

Larry chimed in: "Is he back from Norway yet?"

"Yeah," Kacey said. "Just got back this morning."

"Tell him I said hello," Larry said.

"Will do. He's in the back right now. Maybe I can pull him from what he's doing and have him come out and say hello."

Larry beamed.

"No," Grandma said. "We don't want to bother him if he's busy."

"It's no trouble at all."

"Well, if it's no trouble…" Larry started.

Grandma shot him a look that made him trail off before returning his gaze to the menu, pretending to study it intently.

Emma cut in to avoid the awkward silence that would follow. "So, where's Flo?"

"She has tonight off, so you guys are stuck with me."

Grandma's eyes sparkled. "Oh, Kacey. Miss Gerkins

is a bore compared to you. But don't tell her I said that."
Grandma winked.

A blush blossomed on Kacey's cheeks. "I won't,
Grandma Ruth." Kacey surveyed the table. "So, you guys
want to start with some drinks?"

"Sure," Grandma said, and they went around and
ordered their drinks, all staying non-alcoholic, with
Emma and Larry ordering cola, and Sarah and her
grandma getting the sweet tea.

"Okay, and any appetizers?"Kacey didn't write
anything down, and Sarah wondered how she could
remember all their orders.

Larry was whispering something in Grandma's ear,
and she was nodding.

Grandma cleared her throat and swiveled her head
toward her granddaughters. "Sarah. Emma. Let's get that
dip I was telling you about last night."

Sarah and Emma gave one quick nod each, and
Grandma continued without pause, "Okay then, we'll
have an order of the Spinach and Artichoke Dip with
that special cheese, and an extra order of tortilla chips,
please."

"You got it," Kacey said, then strode off.

Sarah and her family chatted for a few minutes and
then their drinks and appetizers came.

Larry picked up a tortilla chip and scooped up a bit of the delicious-looking dip.

"Lawrence," Grandma said, eyebrows furrowed. "That's an awful lot of dip you're taking. Leave some for the girls."

Larry leaned his chip slightly and half of the dip slid back into the main bowl. He ate a portion of the chip with the dip on it.

"Mmm," he said, eyes closed briefly. He started back down toward the large bowl of dip.

Grandma smacked his hand as it was en route to the bowl. "No double-dipping, Lawrence." Grandma shook her head. "Can't take him anywhere."

Emma giggled softly as Larry crunched away on the rest of his dip-less chip. "Poor Grandpa."

"So," Kacey said, "is everyone ready to order?"

Larry took a sip of his cola, smacked his lips together, and said to his wife, "Ruth, why don't you go first."

"Ah, yes," Grandma said, smiling up at Kacey. "I'll have the Caribbean Chicken Salad."

Sarah peered down at her menu, searching for the choice her grandma made. The salad featured grilled chicken, pecans, cucumbers, and tomatoes atop a bed of chopped greens with sliced avocados on the side.

"With the mango ranch dressing?" Kacey asked.

"Of course."

"And for you?" Kacey asked Emma.

"Cascade Burger, please."

Sarah remembered that the Cascade Burger had American cheese, lettuce, and tomato, and she salivated at the thought.

"Boardwalk fries with that?" Kacey asked.

Emma closed her menu and smiled. "You better believe it."

Kacey scribbled down Emma's order and turned to Sarah, "And you?"

"I'll have the same."

"Good choice, Sarah. And finally, Mr. Shores?"

"I'd like an order of the Fish and Chips, please."

Kacey jotted down Larry's order and pocketed her pen and pad. "You got it," she said, and strode away from their table, like a woman on a mission.

In less than fifteen minutes, Kacey delivered their food, delicious-smelling aromas wafting from each plate.

"Oh my," Larry said upon seeing the plate of fish and French fries, served with tartar sauce. "This looks amazing, as always, Kacey."

"Thanks," Kacey said, setting the rest of the orders on the table. "Anything else I can get for you?" she asked.

Sarah lowered her gaze to the meal, mesmerized for

a second by the double-stacked burger that sat next to a large pile of French fries. She returned her gaze to Kacey, grinning. "I think I'm good."

"Me too," Emma muttered, and Grandma and Grandpa nodded their agreement.

"Okay," Kacey said, "I'll be back to check to see how you're doing."

Kacey hurried off toward another patron who was trying to wave her down, and Sarah saw a muscular man walking toward them. He wore a polo shirt that was mostly concealed by a green apron. She spotted the Banana Hammock logo on the apron as the man came up to their table.

"Well, if it isn't Gary Hammock!" Larry said, reaching his hand out to shake the man's. "How was your trip?"

"Wonderful. How are you?"

"No complaints."

"Just got in myself," Grandma said.

"Is that so, Ruth? Another cruise?"

"Yeah, but I let a colleague grab some of my hours, which worked out, so I could see Sarah here."

Sarah smiled, as her grandma put a hand on her shoulder.

"Sarah! Wow, you look great! How's the job in New York?" Gary said.

Sarah was surprised that Gary would remember, since she hadn't seen him in a long time. "It's going good. Thanks for asking."

"So, how long were you in Norway?" Larry asked.

Gary turned his attention to Larry. "A month. Was visiting family."

"And how are they?"

"Good. I was helping my nephew for most of the time I was over there. He's a scientist with the NPI."

"NPI?" Grandma asked, using her fork to pick at her chicken salad. "What's that?"

"Norwegian Polar Institute, or as the Norwegians call it: Norsk Polarinstitutt," Gary said, the last two words coming out with a faux Scandinavian accent.

Grandma huffed. "I'm still confused."

Gary smiled. "The NPI is a government institution for scientific research; they do mapping, and monitor the environment in the Antarctic and Arctic. They advise the Norwegian authorities on things that deal with the polar environments. I was over there volunteering to help save the polar bears, giving them food and whatnot. It's an annual trip I take."

Larry said, "I bet the climate is different over there..."

"Polar opposites," Gary said, then he and Larry laughed at the joke.

Emma and Grandma exchanged a glance, shaking their heads. "They think they're Abbott and Costello," Grandma said.

"Well, I don't want your food to get cold," Gary said. "Enjoy your meals. And we should get together soon, Larry. It's been a long time."

"Sure thing, Gary. Maybe we could go fishing soon."

Gary beamed. "Yes! We should. My friend has a new place, and he's going there this weekend. He invited me, but I'm sure he wouldn't mind if you came too. He always says, 'The more the merrier.'"

"I say that all the time."

"I know. That's why I think you guys would get along great," Gary said with a smile. "I can talk to him tonight after work and call you with the details."

Larry regarded Grandma and she nodded. "I think that would be wonderful. Larry, dear, you need the break and I need some quality time with my girls."

Larry smiled. "I'm a little nervous leaving the shop but it's been a while since I went fishing with friends." He turned to Gary. "Count me in."

"Great! I'll call you tonight after I talk to Barry. He's going to be thrilled you're coming along."

Gary said his goodbyes and meandered back toward the kitchen. A few moments later, Kacey stopped by the table to see how their meals were.

"Good," Larry said, with everyone nodding in agreement, their mouths mostly full of the delicious food masterfully made by Gary Hammock and his team.

"Excellent," Kacey said. "Hope my dad didn't talk your ears off when he was over here. He tends to do that."

"Bah," Grandma said, "your dad is fine by us. Interesting fellow."

Before Kacey could reply, Sarah's ringtone blared.

Larry's caterpillar eyebrows furrowed. "Hmm. You usually keep that thing on silent every other time, but at dinner…"

Sarah glanced at her phone, the name glowing on her caller ID: Adam Dunkin.

"Excuse me," she said, standing up and stepping away from the table as her family continued eating and chatting with Kacey.

On her way out to the front of the restaurant, she answered the call.

"Hey, Adam."

"Sarah, I need to talk to you."

"About what?"

Adam hesitated, and Sarah wondered what was wrong.

"What's going on?" she asked.

"Listen, Sarah, I need to talk to you in person."

CHAPTER 3

"You can't tell me over the phone, Adam?" Sarah asked, watching a few people enter the Banana Hammock as she stood outside. Her cousin and grandparents were still inside, enjoying their meals.

Sarah pressed the phone to her ear, waiting for a reply.

"No," came Adam's voice. "I'd rather talk to you in person."

Sarah glanced back at her cousin and grandparents through the window of the restaurant. They were enjoying their food and laughing. "I'm out with my family now. I think Grandpa Larry is about to order the volcano cake." Sarah let out a small giggle to lighten the mood.

Adam's stern voice came over the phone. "Stop over to my house tomorrow. Then we can talk."

"All right," Sarah said, scratching her head. She didn't know why Adam was so serious. Whatever he wanted to talk about must've been really important. "Tomorrow it is."

Sarah pocketed her phone and headed back into the restaurant to join her family. Her mood had switched, and she could feel the contrast in the air.

"Everything okay?" Grandma asked, pressing her fork into a piece of chicken. She'd obviously sensed the change in mood.

"Yeah, that was Adam. I'm going to go over to his place tomorrow."

"Ooh," Emma said, winking. "Sounds like fun."

"Not really," Sarah said. "Sounds like he has something serious he wants to tell me in person."

"I wonder what it is," Larry said.

Sarah shrugged. "I don't know, but I guess I'll find out."

They finished their meals and Larry paid the bill. They said goodbye to Kacey, and as they walked out, Sarah spotted Gary Hammock near one of the tables, chatting with another group of people. She waved to them and smiled.

Gary looked up and waved. "I'll be in touch," Gary called out to Larry.

"Those two," Grandma said, shaking her head. "They'll be into trouble before we know it."

Back outside, they crossed the street and made their way back to the apartment.

Rugby and Winston greeted them at the door, and Misty jumped from a spot on the couch and raced back toward one of the bedrooms.

"That cat of yours isn't too sociable," Grandma said to Emma.

"Yeah, I'm not sure what's up with her lately. She has been acting a bit strange," Emma said.

"Maybe we've overstayed our welcome," Sarah chimed in. "She was fine the first week we were here."

"Well, except for the first day," Larry said. "I thought I'd have to call the fire department to get her off the shelf in the boutique!"

Grandma chuckled and strode toward the bookshelf, pulling a scrapbook into her hands. "That cat definitely has a mind of its own."

"Doing some scrapbooking tonight, Grandma?" Sarah asked, moving toward the table in the middle of the room.

"I have some catching up to do, yes."

Larry lumbered toward the master bedroom. "I'm going to go get cleaned up and get ready for bed." Even though it was early in the evening yet, no one questioned him. Larry usually liked to take a shower early and get comfortable while he worked on puzzles or settled in with a book for a couple of hours before lights out.

Grandma shuffled to the table and set the book down, opening it. She eased into the chair, silent as she flipped through the pages.

Emma plopped down on the couch, swinging her feet up. She grabbed a book that was on the coffee table and opened it up to where a bookmark was sticking out. She let out a long breath as she scanned the page, a slight smile on her face as she slid into the story-world.

As everyone started their evening "before bed" routine, Sarah lumbered over toward her grandpa's chair. He let her use it whenever she wanted, and she was grateful—it was the most comfortable seat in the apartment.

She grabbed her knitting needles and observed the work she'd already done on the piece. This time, she was making a dog sweater with a double-cable braid down the back, cuffs for the front legs, and a turtleneck. She was excited about this one, making it with ivory merino wool and alpaca. As she worked, the ribbing on the turtleneck came out real nice, and she had almost reached the leg openings when her eyes got heavy.

Taking a break from her knitting, she leaned back and closed her eyes. Next thing she knew, she was being nudged by her cousin.

"It's getting late," Emma said.

"What time is it?"

"Almost midnight. I know you have to meet Adam tomorrow, so..."

"Thanks, Em." Sarah pulled herself from the comfy chair and padded into the bathroom, careful not to wake her grandparents, who were already snoring away in the bedroom.

A tinge of excitement was in her belly. Tomorrow, she would go to Adam's house, and she wondered what he wanted to tell her. Must've been sensitive information if he wouldn't tell her over the phone. She tried not to think of it. The mystery of it all would keep her up through the night.

The next morning, Sarah and Emma were at the boutique. Grandma and Grandpa Larry were out and about, running errands, and so they were left at the boutique until they got back. Sarah was texting with Adam, asking when she should come over, and he said around lunchtime, while he was on his break, so all she could do was bide time by helping Emma.

"Sarah," Emma said, "could you ring Mr. Keifer out for me while I help Ms. Jones over there?"

"Sure," Sarah said, and she spotted the handsome forty-something man approach the counter with a few items. He was tall and built with broad shoulders and thick arms, like he worked out, and his tanned forehead glistened with sweat.

"How are you, Mr. Keifer? Did you find everything you were looking for?"

"Sure did." He laid his items on the counter. "And please, call me Toby."

Sarah grasped a matching pink leash and color set and started to check the customer out. "Good to hear, Toby. So, how many dogs do you have?"

"Oh, this isn't for me. Just wanted to pick up a few things for my mom's Shih Tzu," he said, grinning.

"How nice of you to run errands for your mom."

"Yeah, well, I owe a lot to her. Wouldn't have my business if she didn't help me over the years."

"Oh, you have a business in the area?"

"I own the crab shack down at the end of the boardwalk."

"Oh, yeah," Sarah said, remembering the crab shack and their logo of a crab above the entryway. "I'm not sure if I've been in there."

"You'll have to stop in sometime. I have fresh fish daily." He puffed out his chest a bit, and Sarah could tell he was proud of his business.

"Do you serve shrimp?"

"We most certainly do," he said, giving her a warm smile as if he were a used-car salesman about to give a lengthy pitch. "We have a wonderful shrimp entree of jumbo shrimp crusted with coconut, fried and served with coconut ranch sauce. Comes with a side of our homemade boardwalk fries."

"Mmm," Sarah said, salivating. "I absolutely love coconut shrimp. I'll definitely have to stop by sometime soon."

Sarah placed the last of Toby's items in a bag and set it on the counter. He handed her his credit card, its shiny gold plastic glinting in the artificial store lights, and she completed ringing him out.

"Please do." He took his credit card and grabbed his bag. "Take care...uh, I don't think I caught your name."

Sarah put out her hand to shake his. "Sarah."

Toby shook her hand. "Nice to meet you. So long, Sarah. Hope to see you soon."

Toby was about to walk out when he was stopped by another man. "Toby, we missed you out in the water last weekend."

"Oh, yeah. I came down with a bug, but I'll be out this weekend," Toby said.

Sarah realized why he looked so tanned. He was a fisherman. Made sense, since he owned a restaurant that sold crab and shrimp.

Toby gave him a pat on the back and made his way out the door, whistling.

The other man made a beeline to Emma. He leaned up against the counter after she finished up with Ms. Jones. "What's shakin', darling?" he said with a wink.

"Your butt will be shaking right out the door if you're not here to purchase something," Emma said.

"Woah, there." The man put his hands up in defense. "Hostile today."

"You'll see hostile."

"All right, all right." The man looked around and took a flea comb from one of the tubs that were on the counter.

Emma chuckled. "I should have known."

The man gave her a confused look.

Emma held up the comb and shot him a look. "Got fleas?"

The man huffed. "There's no winning with you." He walked toward the door, then swept back around. "Emma, you're like a prized fish I'd like to—"

"Finish that sentence, and I'll see to it that you don't ever walk again."

The man smiled and walked out.

Emma always was stunning, and the boys were always tripping over themselves to be with her. But since childhood, she either didn't notice, which probably drove the boys mad, or she was too preoccupied with her computer, building websites and understanding algorithms.

"Who was that?" Sarah asked.

"Erwin Dumphry," Emma said, rolling her eyes. "Football star in his high school. Wouldn't give a girl like me the time of day until after graduation, when his cheerleader girlfriends moved on and are now knocked up by some new losers." Emma shook her head. "Complete blockhead who now works for his dad as a fisherman."

Sarah chuckled. "You sure attract some winners."

"Like bees to honey," Emma said.

A few more customers came and went, and Sarah and

Emma worked together to help everyone find exactly what they were looking for. She'd even sold a few of her knitted dog sweaters, and with each one she rang out, she felt the satisfaction that came with someone appreciating her handiwork. Her grandpa would surely try to give her a cut of the proceeds, though she would deny it, as usual. Keeping their business afloat and humming along was more important to her than getting a few extra dollars.

After a couple more hours, Sarah's gaze shifted to the clock on the wall, and she saw that it was quarter to noon.

"I have to go meet Adam," she said to Emma.

"Go ahead. I'll hold down the fort until Grandma and Grandpa get back. They shouldn't be too much longer—they know you have a date."

"It's not a date."

"Suuuure."

Sarah swatted her cousin, tapping her lightly. Of course, she would think it was a date. Sarah and Adam went back a long way, but it was all platonic. Though he was just her type, she didn't want to risk their friendship. He meant way too much to her.

"Okay," Sarah said, stepping out from behind the counter. She smacked the palms of her hands against her thighs a few times, and Rugby and Winston came prancing out from their sleeping spots. "Want to go to Adam's?"

Both dogs responded by sitting nicely, looking up at her expectantly.

As Sarah leashed them up, Emma said, "You're taking the dogs?"

Sarah looked up as she was leashing Rugby. "Yeah, of course I am. Adam has that big, fenced-in yard. No way I'm going to pass up a chance to give these guys some much-needed exercise."

"I'm sure Rugby will have a ball with Winston there," Emma said, taking a seat on the stool behind the counter.

"Yeah, it'll be Winston's first visit. I can't wait to see them play together in a big yard." Sarah smiled.

"Well, you all have fun, then. Misty and I will be bustling here, getting work done."

Misty's eyes opened at the sound of her name. She looked like a jumbo ball of fur with eyes when she lay curled up in her spot on the shelf. She gave a yawn and nestled her head back into the pile of puff. Sarah could hear her purr from where she stood.

"Yeah, looks like Misty is ready to get busy." Sarah laughed.

Emma shook her head. "Well, she's good for moral support."

Sarah laughed again, and the dogs pulled her toward the door. "Well, gotta go," Sarah said. "Don't want to be late—"

"—for your date."

Sarah ignored her cousin's snickering, her mind too focused on the mystery of what Adam wanted to discuss. Soon, she'd find out.

CHAPTER 4

*C*ruising down the main strip of Cascade Cove, the warm air swept through Sarah's hair, and she headed to the outskirts of town where Adam lived.

She pulled into his driveway and saw his house. It was a majestic, two-story Victorian house with blue shutters and several flower boxes in the windows that Adam kept lively. It was his grandmother's house, and she allowed him to live in it while she moved out to California. Her moving was bittersweet for both of them. His grandmother had always loved the California sun and couldn't wait to live there when she retired. For Adam, he was just happy that his grandmother got to live her dream but was sad to see her go. She gave him the house with the promise that she could stay there with him when she came to visit. He was her only grandson, and she adored him, visiting from time to time, which was usually in the off-season when she could relax and spend quality time with her him. This also gave her a chance to visit Sarah's grandmother. They had become good friends after Sarah and Adam met on the beach that blissful summer.

Sarah headed toward the front door, with Rugby pulling her and Winston in tow, and before she got there, Adam appeared from around the side of the house.

"Hey, Sarah, bring the dogs around this way."

He led her into the back yard, opening the gate to the white picket fence, so she and her furry companions could enter.

"I love it back here," she said, looking at the large yard, probably at least an acre of space. "It's always so beautiful."

"Thanks."

He motioned toward a table on the back patio that overlooked the yard. She let Rugby and Winston off their leashes, and they bounded around the yard. Rugby caught sight of something in the corner of the fence—a squirrel or chipmunk or something—and he raced toward it, but it scurried under the fence before he could reach where it had been.

Sarah sat down at the table and scanned the mess of

folders and papers strewn about. "What's all this?"

"Stuff from work."

"Bringing your work home now?"

"Always have. I get some of my best work done out here, where there are no disruptions."

Rugby barked at something, and Winston followed suit.

"Until now," she said.

"Yeah, until now…But this is where a lot of the magic happens. Some of my best thinking on the Jacobs case was done here."

"Are you still in trouble over that?"

"Well, they did give me a promotion and got me off desk duty, but I got a slap on the wrist for what we did."

Sarah's cheeks flushed slightly. "Sorry about that."

"Don't be." Adam picked up a folder, opening it to view the contents. He closed it and threw the folder back down onto the table.

"What's this?" Sarah asked, looking at the folder.

"You know the murder at Cecil's B&B?"

"So, it *is* a murder?"

"Yes. The victim is Frederick Critsworth, a food critic that only comes into town annually. Known as 'Cruel Critsworth.' Apparently, he's a restaurant critic. A very unlikable one that has many enemies. This is the file."

"The file?"

"Yeah. It's everything we have so far."

Sarah opened the file and leafed through the papers, noticing some photos that she figured had been taken at the crime scene.

Adam said, "Well, it seems as though we've hit a wall."

"Oh yeah?" Sarah said, still ruffling through the many papers and pictures.

"Yeah, a dead end."

Sarah pulled out a picture and studied it. "What about this?"

Still staring at the photo, she realized it was a picture of a partial footprint with what appeared to be a logo. She pulled out her cell phone, making it look like she was checking a message, but instead snapped a picture of the photograph.

"This logo looks like some sort of animal," Sarah said, handing the picture to Adam.

"Oh, that. Those are just pictures taken around the perimeter of the B&B. It's standard protocol that we snap shots of whatever we find. But those prints, they don't really mean anything. There were so many people that went in and out of the B&B before and after the murder."

"Oh."

"Yeah, and we've been trying to keep the murder quiet, as to not frighten the tourists."

That made sense. Tourists were how Cascade Cove operated. Without them, all the business owners would have nothing, since the tourist season was the primary way they made any sort of money.

Adam continued, "All we know is that the victim died last Saturday, sometime around ten p.m. There was no forced entry, and it appears that the victim was strangled."

"Strangled? Do you have a murder weapon?"

"No. We found nothing in the room, and we checked the entire B&B."

"Hmm. Maybe it was done with rope or a telephone cord..."

Adam shook his head. "No, nothing like that. There were no rope burns, so we ruled that out, and the ligature marks look nothing like a telephone cord. The marks show that they used something thinner. Like a wire or something."

Sarah gasped and put her fingers to her lips, as a warm breeze swept across the patio. "Did anyone see or hear anything?"

"No, and Cecil doesn't have proper cameras installed. It's a small B&B, and he didn't think he'd need one in a small, beachside town like Cascade Cove. At this point, with no more leads and no witnesses, we're not sure how to proceed."

Sarah shook her head. "This is horrible."

"Yeah, and that's not it."

"Oh?"

"There was an anonymous phone call to the police at ten p.m. that night. A woman. She found the body and called it in. The 911 operator couldn't keep her on the phone. She just hung up and was nowhere to be found after."

"That's strange. Most people want to help."

"I know. We really need to figure this out, though, and soon. I'm not sure how much longer we can go like this before we lose tourists. You know how rumors are around here. The people of Cascade Cove are already talking about it, and if tourists start catching wind of this death being an actual murder…"

Adam didn't have to finish the sentence. Sarah knew what this would mean for Cascade Cove.

"So," Adam continued, "I called you yesterday because I wanted to ask you a favor."

"What is it?"

"The other day, your grandma said that Larry and Cecil go way back. I was thinking maybe you can go talk to Cecil."

"But you got in trouble the last time I got involved."

"We also solved a case that otherwise would not have been solved if you didn't get involved. Besides, like I said, it was a slap on the wrist, and we also got a lot of praise."

Sarah's lips were pursed, and she ignored the sounds of Rugby and Winston barking off at the other end of the yard. They were in their own world, where murders and crime didn't exist. A much simpler life...

"Just talk to him and see if he says anything that may lead us to something," Adam said, breaking Sarah's thoughts.

"You want me to question him?"

"No, no. Just talk to him. Tell him you're Larry's granddaughter. People seem to talk more when they're comfortable and maybe he will spill something that will help."

"I don't know. I'm not sure I want to—"

"It will be for Cascade Cove, Sarah. For your grandparents." Adam focused his gaze on the scattered papers, a somber look on his face. "And to get justice for Frederick."

Sarah took a deep breath.

"Can I have some time to think about it?" she asked.

Adam hesitated. "Sure. But, Sarah, we don't have much time."

CHAPTER 5

*L*ater that day, Sarah was back at the apartment with her cousin and grandparents. Larry was in the kitchen cooking, while Emma and Grandma were stationed at the table, going through the scrapbooks.

Sarah was lounging in the comfy chair, knitting. She took a deep breath and smelled the fish Larry was frying in the kitchen, and her stomach rumbled softly. Despite her hunger, she was intent on continuing her knitting—it allowed for her to multitask the creation of new product with the ability to get some deep-level thinking in, and at the moment, she had a lot to think about.

Did she want to get involved in another investigation? She knew that Adam was at a dead-end, but she questioned the wisdom of her getting wrapped up in another murder case.

It had been risky last time, and she didn't think it would be wise to take such a risk a second time around.

She furrowed her brow, thinking it over as she mindlessly knitted.

Emma was heading to the bookshelf to get another scrapbook and turned to look at Sarah.

"What's wrong?" Emma asked.

"Nothing." Sarah's knitting needles were clanking faster and more furiously.

"Oh, come on. What's going on?"

"I said, nothing." Sarah looped the yarn over her right needle and tried to pass it under, but it slipped. She dropped a stitch and grumbled.

Emma planted her hands on her hip. "Oh, really?" she said. "Does it have anything to do with what you went to talk to Adam about?"

Sarah let out a long breath, her knitting needles clinking together as she worked. It only took a moment to fix the dropped stitch and move on.

Emma took a step closer. "It is, isn't it? Tell me what happened."

Grandma came over to where Emma was standing and shook her head. "I could have gotten it myself, you know?" Grandma's gaze turned to Sarah, and she cocked her head. "What's wrong with her?"

"I don't know," Emma said. "She went to talk to Adam, and now she's acting all weird."

Sarah set her needles down and gave her grandma and cousin each a cursory glance. She took another deep breath, the smell of fish potent in her nostrils. Her stomach rumbled again, but she ignored it. "I'm not acting weird."

Emma's eyes crinkled. "Yeah, right."

"Fine. I'll tell you what happened. He wants me to get involved with the murder investigation, that's what happened."

"So, it is a murder, then," Larry called from the kitchen.

Sarah craned her neck to look over at Larry. The man had bionic ears or something. Her whole family did when it came to gossip, so she wasn't surprised. "Yeah. And Adam wants me to talk to your friend, Cecil. Says that people trust me and that I might be able to help him and his colleagues get unstuck in their investigation."

"Cecil's a swell guy," Larry said, nodding.

"That's what I heard. So why can't you go talk to him, Grandpa?" Sarah asked. "I'm sure he'd talk to you, and you could help Adam."

"I don't have time for that. I have to get ready."

"For what?"

Grandma answered for him, "He and Gary are going on that fishing trip together this weekend with..." Grandma snapped her fingers as she racked her brain for a name.

"Barry," Larry called from the kitchen.

"Yeah, that's right. Barry, Gary, and Larry. Sounds like quite the trio, if you ask me." Grandma let out a chuckle.

"Oh, drat!" Larry said, pots clanging.

"Please, Lawrence. Not another incident."

"Everything's okay. Nothing to see here."

Grandma marched into the kitchen. "Oh, Lawrence! You spilled an entire container of salt!"

"There still some in the shaker in the cabinet."

"What were you doing with the whole container? You only need a pinch." Grandma huffed. "Well, this can't be good, especially right before a fishing trip."

"I didn't spill it on the fish. It's fine. I'd say that's pretty lucky."

Grandma clicked her tongue at him. "I'll get this cleaned up while you finish dinner."

"Get ready to eat, girls," Larry called out. "Dinner will be ready in a minute."

The smell of fried fish and mashed potatoes wafted from the kitchen, and Sarah couldn't help her body from propelling from the chair. Once out of the chair, Sarah followed Emma and Grandma over to the table to take a seat.

Sarah eased into the chair, and eyed Emma, who was grabbing a fork and knife in preparation for their feast.

"Smells good, Grandpa," Emma said, eyeing up one of the serving plates Larry carried to the table.

Larry placed the plate down on the table. "Fried haddock with green beans and my famous garlic mashed potatoes. There's also a surprise dessert in the kitchen, courtesy of your grandma."

Sarah picked up a napkin and placed it across her lap, remaining silent as Rugby and Winston played in the living room, yapping away.

"That's enough, guys," Emma said, pressing a couple fingers against her temple as if she were suffering a headache. She shot Sarah a quick glance. "Notice Misty isn't causing a ruckus."

Sarah cut into her haddock and took a bite. "Nope." Sarah pointed her fork toward Misty on the floor. She appeared to be on edge, claws digging into the carpet. "But Rugby and Winston will get to her soon."

Just then, Rugby waltzed over to her and gave her a sloppy, wet kiss on the side of her head. Misty hissed and took off. Sarah and everyone burst into laughter.

"Better dinner entertainment than the TV," Larry said.

Emma fixed her gaze on Larry. "So, Grandpa, will you be away all weekend?"

"Yeah."

"But Grandma won't be here long before she goes away for work again. Plus, I'm going to be overwhelmed at the store, if Sarah is helping Adam and all. Can't your trip wait?"

"It's okay, dear," Grandma said, placing a hand on Emma's shoulder. "This will give us some quality time together. And I'll help where I can at the store."

"But you don't even know how to work the register," Emma said.

Grandma put a finger to her chin. "Well, it can't be that hard."

Emma scoffed. "Grandma, I can't even teach you how to use a cell phone."

"I just want to dial a phone number, Emma." Grandma furrowed her brow. "I just don't understand why those things have to be so darn complicated. It's supposed to be a phone, after all. And besides, I used to be a cashier at a grocery store when I was a teenager. How much could a register change over the years?"

"You know, Grandma, the register is now a computer," Sarah said.

"Oh," Grandma said, waving her hand at the comment. "I know computers. I check my emails, and Emma helped set me up on that photobook website." Grandma paused a second, thinking. "Or is it friendbook?"

Emma rubbed her temples again and flashed a look at Sarah. Sarah stifled a laugh and shrugged.

"Fine," Emma said, returning her gaze to Grandma. "I'll teach you the register. It's really not that hard and, apparently, you're my only hope."

"That's the spirit," Larry said, smiling. "Now that you have that figured out, I'm going to go get Grandma's special strawberry shortcake cupcakes."

Sarah's mouth watered. One of her all-time favorite desserts was Grandma's strawberry shortcake cupcakes. They were fluffy vanilla cake stuffed with strawberry filling and topped with a light whipped cream with strawberry bits swirled in. Every bite was heavenly. No —magical.

Larry came in with the tray of delicious cupcakes and set them down in the middle of the table. Sarah couldn't help but eye them while she was finishing her dinner.

"So, you're going to talk to Cecil, Sarah?" Larry asked. "Tell him I'll be in touch. A round of bowling may be in order," Larry said with a wink.

Sarah said, "I'm not sure I want to go to—"

"Bah, what's the harm in talking to the man?" Grandma said. "And from what I heard, you did a lot to help Adam with the whole Jacobs case. You're a natural sleuth, sweetie, so why not help the boy out?"

Sarah picked at her haddock for a moment, finally deciding to take a bite of the mashed potatoes instead. "Well," she said between bites, "I would, but I don't want Adam to get in trouble again at the station."

"I understand," Grandma said, "but maybe you could just help Adam to get unstuck using your people skills and that'll be that. You always had a way with people, and folks like Cecil have practically watched you grow up over the years. I'm sure he'd love it if you visited him."

Sarah smiled. "Maybe under different circumstances…"

"Well, yeah…A murder at his B&B is pretty traumatic, but still…"

Sarah shook her head.

Emma clapped her hands. "C'mon, Sarah, we could put some baddies away," she said.

Sarah took a bite of her haddock and shook her head again. "Don't get too far ahead of yourself. I said I might go talk to him. Besides, weren't you just complaining how you were going to be too busy at the boutique? I can't say we're going to morph into those amateur sleuths in the mystery novels you read."

Emma chuckled. "Well, were not a 24-hour convenience store. I could still help. And you never know. You might become a real-life Nancy Drew."

"Or you could both be like the Hardy Boys." Larry smiled. "I was more of a Hardy Boys fan myself, back in the day."

"He used to have a whole collection of those books when I first met him," Grandma said, halfway finished with her meal.

"You know, I still have a first edition copy of *The Tower Treasure*."

"The first in the series?" Emma asked. "I didn't know you had that."

"Sure do," Larry said. "It's on the bookshelf over there. But if you're into the Nancy Drew books, I have a copy of *The Secret of the Old Clock*, too, though it's not a first edition."

Emma smiled. "Looks like I'll be steeped in nostalgia tonight."

Sarah grabbed one of the cupcakes sitting in the middle of the table and undressed it. She took a sizable bite, savoring the soft cake and creamy strawberry filling inside. Her eyes fluttered closed for a second as she took in the texture and flavor of the sugary dessert, lost in her own nostalgia for a moment.

After they finished their meals, everyone helped clean up and Sarah excused herself, so she could call Adam.

She retreated into the bedroom she shared with her cousin and closed the door.

Before she could grab her cell phone, Emma poked her head in.

"What's up, Em?"

"I just wanted to see if you were going to call your boyfriend."

Sarah put her hands on her hips. "He's not my boyfriend."

"Well, I know how to get a rise out of you," Emma said. "So, are you going to talk to Cecil?"

"I don't know yet."

"At dinner you said you would."

"I said I'd think about it. That's what I'm doing now…"

Emma came into the room and plopped down on the bed. "Just think, you'll help to get a killer off the streets while simultaneously helping every small business owner in town from losing customers. Once word gets out that there's a killer on the loose, all the tourists who just flooded in will be flooding out."

"I know."

"And don't forget, Grandma and Grandpa will be victims in all this. We need all the sales we can get if we want a chance at advertising properly for the website, not to mention getting things in order for Grandpa's new product line."

"You don't think I've considered all of that?"

"I know you have, but a little reminder couldn't hurt."

"Shameless reminder, if you ask me."

"You're being dramatic. Just help Adam by talking to Cecil."

"Go read some Nancy Drew or something," Sarah said, swatting her cousin away.

Sarah pulled her phone from her pocket and gripped it tightly as she sat on her bed. She was still apprehensive about getting involved. Sure, she could get justice for Frederick Critsworth while helping her grandparents and all the other business owners in the area. But she couldn't shake the dread—a real life killer could grow privy to her activities if she weren't careful. And that could put her and the rest of her family at risk.

"I can't do it," she said aloud. "I'll just tell him I'm not comfortable getting involved. He'll understand."

Sitting alone in the room, the words reverberated in her mind.

He'll understand...

Of course, but would she be able to live with herself?

If this case dragged on, and in the meantime, business in Cascade Cove dried up, would she be able to look herself in the mirror?

She'd solved one crime before. Why not another?

But her mind circled back to the risks involved.

For ten minutes, she deliberated, putting the phone down on her bed, then picking it back up again. Half-tempted to go back out to her grandpa's comfy chair and resume her knitting, she picked up her phone one last time, ready to turn it off for the night.

But instead of turning it off, she dialed Adam and heard it ring twice in her ear. Before the third ring, he answered the call.

"What's up?"

Sarah cleared her throat. "About what we were talking about..."

"So," Adam said, tone serious, "what did you decide?"

"I'll do it," Sarah said into the phone.

Adam's reply was immediate. "Good! When will you be talking to Cecil?"

"I'll go over tomorrow morning."

"Thanks, Sarah." She could hear the relief in his voice. "And remember..."

"I know, I know...Be discreet."

"Okay. Well, work those secret ninja skills and let me know what you find out."

Sarah let out a chuckle. "Of course," she said.

They said their goodbyes and Sarah laid her phone on her nightstand and plugged it in to charge. Tomorrow would be a big day. She could sense it.

CHAPTER 6

The next morning, Sarah got up and took a shower. Afterward, she padded to her luggage and unzipped it. She hadn't put any clothes away since she had expected to only stay two weeks. She had a system: clean clothes from the luggage, dirty clothes in a bag for washing when she got home. There was no point in spending the time to put them in drawers. But now, she didn't have much of an excuse for not putting her clothes away, since Grandma had already found her bag of dirty clothes and cleaned them. And then there was the fact that she was staying much longer than two weeks. So, chalk it up to laziness, Sarah thought. Besides, her cousin was enjoying having all the drawer and closet space.

She kept digging until she found a denim tunic and a

pair of white capris. She decided to pull her hair back, and slipped on her blue canvas boat shoes, before heading out the door.

Out in the living room, she saw her grandma and grandpa hugging.

"You be safe, Lawrence." Grandma swiped her hand across his shoulder, pulling lint or something from his Hawaiian shirt. "Do you have your toothbrush?"

"Nah," he said, grin splashed across his face. "Decided I'd just let my dental hygiene go this weekend."

"Oh, Lawrence." Grandma chuckled. "Do you have your cell phone?"

"I do, but Barry said that there won't be any reception out there."

Grandma grimaced.

Larry shifted his weight to one side. "Well, you don't have reception when you're off working on the cruise almost every week."

"You're right, Lawrence." Grandma gave him one final hug. "I love you."

"Love you, too," Larry said, ending their embrace.

Grandma gave him a kiss and then rubbed her ruby-red lipstick off his face.

It was now Sarah's turn to give Larry a hug. "See you soon," he said to her, then he gave Emma a hug and pet each of the animals in turn. "Rugby, Winston, Misty... you all behave."

Emma beamed. "I know Misty will...not sure about those two."

"Well, I better get to the bus terminal." Larry glanced at his watch. "Oh boy. I'm going to be late."

After Larry was gone, Sarah soon left the apartment as well, saying goodbye to Grandma and Emma as she went, and made her way down the steps and out the building. She strode along the sidewalk and got into her Corolla.

She started off down the road, pulled a U-turn, and drove south on the main strip, down toward where the amusement park and the Ferris wheel were. The Ferris wheel was in motion, and she noticed that it was only at half capacity. That night, it would probably be full.

At the edge of town, she spotted the sign for the Beachside Bed and Breakfast off to her right. Cecil's place.

She pulled into the gravel parking lot and parked next to a tan Oldsmobile Cutlass Supreme. It looked like something an old man would drive, and she figured it was Cecil's.

"This thing's probably older than I am," Sarah said, regarding the relic automobile, though she was sure it wasn't quite as old as Grandpa's Pinto.

Then she eyed the B&B, and the Oldsmobile no longer seemed ancient. The elegant Queen Anne-style mansion stood before her, and she could only imagine how charming the inside was, if the exterior were any indication.

She exited her Corolla and the gravel crunched beneath her feet as she stepped toward the hulking structure that featured a wrap-around porch.

"My goodness."

She'd driven past the B&B frequently but hadn't seen it up this close. Excitedly, she strode along the walkway, flanked with two-foot-tall shrubs, and made her way up onto the porch. She rapped on the front door and waited.

When nobody answered, she knocked again.

"Come on in," came a strained voice.

Sarah let herself in, and saw a man sitting in a leather chair on the other end of the large, lavishly decorated room. There was a sitting area near an inactive fireplace, and several mahogany bookcases filled with more titles than Sarah could count.

"Hello there," Sarah said, smiling at the man.

He rose from his chair, holding a book in one hand and a cane in the other. He wore a tan-colored fedora, its brim a half-inch away from the top of his gray eyebrows. The man's smile reached his eyes, and the wrinkles were apparent on his face. He wore a burgundy and white vertically striped dress shirt tucked into a pair of gray pinstripe slacks.

"Sorry, ma'am, but we are closed until further notice," the man said, using his cane as he ambled closer to her.

"Are you Cecil?" she asked.

"That's what they call me."

"I'm Sarah. Larry Shores's granddaughter."

Cecil beamed. "Ah, that son-of-a-gun! How's he lately? Still causing trouble?"

"Always," Sarah said. "Heard you two had a bowling team."

The man's lips wrinkled into a grin, steeped in nostalgia. "The Rock Lobsters. I miss those days..."

"Yeah, so why are you closed?"

"Word hasn't hit your ears yet?"

"It has."

"Then you know why we're closed. It's a shame what happened, and my wife and I are hoping we can open up soon, and that people will still want to stay here."

"I'm sure they will," Sarah said.

For a moment, Sarah thought that perhaps Cecil himself could be a suspect, but the rational part of her mind quickly stomped that theory down as ludicrous. Cecil was the furthest thing from a suspect. As an old man, he wouldn't have had the strength to strangle a man, not to mention the fact that any death at his B&B would be devastating, let alone a murder. So, even though he had the opportunity, he had no means, and certainly no motive. Plus, her grandpa was a character witness in all of this, since he had known Cecil a long time, and he adored the old man.

"If this thing can get solved, then I think we'll be okay," Cecil said. "A lengthy investigation is what I fear the most."

"So, what do you remember about the man who died here?"

"Mr. Critsworth was in the area for the week. He's a restaurant critic, you know?"

"Yeah. I heard he wasn't too kind to the many places he's reviewed."

Cecil laughed. "You get the Understatement of the Year Award! He was despised by many—I'm not surprised someone offed him. I just wish they didn't do it here. But anyway, he was in the area for his work, and also to attend the Tenth Annual Cascade Mixer."

"Like a gala?"

"Yeah, all the prominent people in the area attend it, Frederick Critsworth among them."

"When was it?"

"Funny thing, he went out to attend the mixer, then

poof—dead in his room. We didn't know anything happened until the police showed up."

Suddenly, a middle-aged woman strode into the room, carrying a bucket that was filled with cleaning supplies.

"Mr. Brown," the woman said to Cecil, "may I have a word with you?"

"Excuse me," Cecil said to Sarah.

"Sure. Do you mind if I have a look around?"

"Go right ahead," he said.

Sarah stepped away from the old man and the woman, and strode out of the room. She found the stairs that led up to the second floor. She crept up the steps, waiting for Cecil to say it was off limits, but he was apparently too busy talking with the woman. Their voices carried through the house, though by the time Sarah reached the top of the steps, their conversation was no more than a murmur.

Down the hallway, Sarah spotted a few doors, all labeled with elegant plaques.

"Lighthouse Room," Sarah muttered, reading the first plaque.

She edged down the hallway to the next room.

"Starfish Room."

Near the end of the hallway, off to the right, she saw

another door, the yellow crime scene tape looking out of place across the dark wooden door.

"Sea Breeze Room."

She stared at the plaque, its elegant gold trim glinting in the light cast by the sun shining through a window at the end of the hallway.

A noise at the stairs.

Sarah spun around and spotted the woman who'd been talking to Cecil.

"Sorry," Sarah said. "I didn't—"

"Don't worry," the woman said. "I was just coming up here to grab something."

"Are you the maid here?"

"Yeah, though I won't be cleaning that room anytime soon," she said, pointing at the Sea Breeze Room.

"I guess not. Do you remember anything from the night Mr. Critsworth was murdered?" Sarah asked, throwing discretion to the curb for a moment.

"No," the woman said, then glanced at the Starfish Room, holding her gaze a bit too long.

"What happened in that room?" Sarah asked.

"Nothing."

"You can tell me. I'm just curious."

The maid locked eyes with Sarah, a worried look washing over her face. "I overheard a man in the Starfish

Room say that he would strangle Frederick the night before the murder."

"Why did he want to strangle him?"

"I don't know. I just heard him say 'I'll strangle Frederick for what he did.'"

"Did you tell the police about what you heard?"

"No. I couldn't tell them."

"Why not?"

The maid hesitated for a moment, looking away. Her voice came out small: "Because I have skeletons in my closet. They have a warrant out for my arrest. I can't. I just can't."

"What happened? It's okay."

"No, no...it's not okay. I'm a single mom with four kids. My license is suspended, and they have a warrant out for my arrest. Please don't tell the police. I just wanted to let someone know what I heard, so I could get it off my chest."

"I understand. I won't tell anyone. So, have you seen the man?"

"No, all residents that night were moved to the Dolphin Motel."

"I see."

Sarah remembered the Dolphin Motel, which wasn't too far from her grandpa's boutique in the middle of town.

Then Sarah's mind drifted to the anonymous phone call to the police. Maybe it was the maid, after all...

"I just have one last question, if you don't mind," Sarah said.

"Sure."

"Did you call in the murder that night?"

"No. The police were already here before I knew anything about it."

Sarah pursed her lips and glanced over at the plaque for the Starfish Room. "Do you know who was staying in that room?" she asked the maid.

"Yeah, a realtor and his wife."

"Do you happen to know their names?"

Sarah waited as the maid took in a deep breath, then let it out slowly. She furrowed her brow as if in deep concentration. The seconds ticked by as Sarah waited for that crucial piece of information to be revealed.

Finally, the maid regarded Sarah and said, "Now I remember: Mr. and Mrs. Montgomery."

"Mr. and Mrs. Montgomery?" Sarah asked the maid.

"Yeah, that's who was staying there."

"And they're at the Dolphin Motel now?"

"Yeah."

"Thanks for the info."

Sarah said her goodbyes to the maid and descended the steps, intent on tracking down the realtor named

Mr. Montgomery. A clear threat had been overheard by the maid, the method of the threat matching exactly what had happened to the victim, and Sarah couldn't wait to interview the man.

Once she was downstairs, she thanked Cecil and let herself out.

Back in her Corolla, she drove out of the gravel parking lot and back out onto the main road. As she drove, she thought about everything she had learned so far.

"Why would Mr. Montgomery, a realtor, want a restaurant critic dead?" she said aloud. "What could his motive possibly be?"

That question was what she wanted to find out. The man had the opportunity, since he was staying in a neighboring room, and he probably had the means. But did he have any sort of real motive?

CHAPTER 7

*I*n the middle of town, Sarah pulled into the parking lot for the Dolphin Motel.

Compared to Cecil's B&B, the motel was dingy, though Sarah figured all the other places in the area were likely booked up and this had been a "last resort."

After parking, she got out and walked the property. She checked with the receptionist, asking if she knew where Mr. Montgomery was. The woman was pleasant, though her answer didn't please Sarah much. She learned that she hadn't seen the man, though she'd spotted his wife out at the pool.

Sarah made her way around the back of the motel. She spotted the in-ground pool and a woman leaning all the way back in a lounge chair, sunbathing.

She wore a brimmed hat, sunglasses, and a one-piece, black and white, polka-dotted bathing suit.

Sarah smiled at the woman. "Mrs. Montgomery?"

"Yes?"

"My name is Sarah Shores. I'm Larry's granddaughter."

Mrs. Montgomery lifted her sunglasses a bit, squinting. "Sorry, dear, I don't know a Larry." She returned her glasses to their original position and readjusted herself on the chair. "Could you be a dear and move a smidgen to the left? You're blocking my sun."

"Oh, sorry," Sarah said, moving to the side a bit. "Uh, maybe you know his wife—my grandmother—Ruth Shores?

"Oh, Ruth. Why, yes. My cruise line lady. How is she? She makes killer brownies, and those cupcakes..." Mrs. Montgomery paused for a moment, most likely trying to recapture the taste of the desserts. "Let's just say, they're bad news for my figure."

"She's doing well. She said she missed the mixer the other night. Were you at that party?"

Mrs. Montgomery laid there, soaking up the sun. She didn't look at Sarah as she said, "I was at a party that night. It's a shame Ruth wasn't there."

"Yeah. Did your husband go too?"

"I don't know. I don't keep tabs on him."

Sarah was taken aback by her response. How could she not know if her husband had attended a gala with her? Sarah tried her best to not sound suspicious. "I see," she decided to redirect. "Do you happen to know Mr. Critsworth?"

"The man who was murdered? Why, yes, of course. He was in town for the same party. I guess he was supposed to write some reviews or something, too, while he was here. What a shame."

Sarah cleared her throat, ready to get right to the point: "That night, someone overheard your husband say he would strangle him."

Mrs. Montgomery pulled her back off the chair and turned toward Sarah. She lifted her glasses and rested them atop of her head, a surprised look splashed across her face. Sarah was unsure if she was about to yell at her or if she had just had a revelation.

The woman's mouth dropped slightly. "As a matter of fact, he did say that. Yes, we were having a disagreement...well, you don't think...?"

"Where's your husband now?"

"Probably drowning his sorrows again."

"At the bar?"

"Practically lives there."

"Which one?"

"At Teek's Tiki Bar."

"At Teek's?" The words slipped out an octave higher than she'd expected and before she had a chance to stop herself. She could only imagine what she sounded like from Mrs. Montgomery's point of view.

Mrs. Montgomery let out a slight chuckle as she readjusted herself, laying back and pulling her sunglasses back down. "My, did I strike a nerve, dear?"

"No." Sarah smiled. "Of course not."

"Either you've seen a ghost, or an old flame has been ignited."

Sarah waved both her hands in front of her. "No, no. Nothing like that." In truth, it wasn't anything like that, but the guilt remained the same. He was an old friend. One with history. One that Adam wasn't fond of. Still, it was nothing. She was just surprised to hear his name after so many years.

A bright, painted smile spread across Mrs. Montgomery's face, and Sarah wished she could see her eyes through the dark shades. She wanted to know if she was at least somewhat convincing.

"Listen, dear," Mrs. Montgomery said, "I hate to cut this short, but I'm not one for small talk, and I'm in the middle of a hot date."

Sarah gave a confused look.

Mrs. Montgomery pointed at the sun. "If you don't mind."

"Yeah, of course." Sarah took a step back. "I'll let you get back to your sunbathing."

Mrs. Montgomery didn't say another word and Sarah knew that was her sign that the conversation was now over. So, she turned and started making her way back to the lobby. Her mind was running fast, but she knew where her next stop would be.

Teek's Tiki Bar.

CHAPTER 8

*S*arah left the Dolphin Motel, getting back into her Corolla. A wave of excitement and a tinge of nervousness swelled in her chest at the anticipation of seeing an old friend and questioning a man who could be guilty of murder. Her mind was running in circles.

She drove out of the parking lot and found that her regular spot near her grandparents' boutique was open. She parked in the spot and got out, walking toward the boutique. Instead of actually going through the boutique —in fear of Emma putting her to work—Sarah took a walkway between the buildings that led back to the boardwalk.

She mused for a moment about how unusual it was

walking without dogs. Something about it felt freeing, yet it did make her a tad lonely.

But she was only lonely for so long. On the boardwalk, she saw people everywhere. They were enjoying the day in the afternoon sun. People walked dogs, skateboarders careened about, and beyond the boardwalk—on the beach—someone was flying a kite.

A couple, each holding a baked good, walked past her, the smell of their delicacies making its way into her nose. It was some sort of sticky bun, and the smell of it tempted Sarah to stop for her own.

But she resisted the urge and continued on down the boardwalk.

The sounds of waves crashing off to her left caught her attention, and she spotted motion, but it was only a group of children rushing around, dodging the water that rolled onto the shore. They screamed each time their feet caught the cold touch of the water, but their laughter made her smile.

She remembered when she was young. She and Emma would join Adam and a few other friends to play on the beach like that. They'd fly kites and build sandcastles and go boogie boarding. The thought of those days sent a tingle of nostalgia through her mind. How she missed those days. She let out a sigh and tried to regain her focus.

Up ahead, she spotted the sign for Teek's, though if the man had wanted the outside to scream "tiki bar," he'd utterly failed. It looked more like a bookstore than a tiki bar.

Sarah opened the door to Teek's and the sounds of the boardwalk behind her melted away. Before her was a tiny room, nothing more than a walk-in closet, and Sarah furrowed her brow. It definitely appeared much larger from the outside. A man in a twenties-style suit was stationed behind a small, dark table, giving her a single curt nod. There was a red velvet curtain behind him that swayed from an air source somewhere.

"Is this Teek's?"

"It is," the man said.

Sarah scanned the room, but only saw a few bookshelves lining the walls. There were ancient-looking titles on the shelves, and Sarah gave another quizzical look.

"Are you looking for anything in particular?" the man asked.

Sarah furrowed her eyebrows. "Is this some kind of joke?" She didn't mean to come off as rude, but more confused.

"Is what a joke?"

"Where's Teek?" Sarah asked, on her tiptoes, craning her neck to see if she could catch a peek of what was behind the moving curtains. Maybe it wasn't the same Teek she knew. But how many people were named Teek? Besides, she knew that he had opened his own bar at least a year ago. This had to be the place. "I thought this was supposed to be a bar. You know, where you can buy a drink."

The man raised his eyebrows. "So, you're here for *that*?"

"For what?"

"Exactly." The man reached toward the velvet curtain and pulled it back, revealing a door. "But before you enter, sign this." He pulled out a thick book from under the table.

Sarah eyed the man suspiciously.

"Don't worry, we won't show the authorities," he said.

The word "Guestbook" was printed in gold on the cover of the massive book. The man motioned to the feathered, fountain pen and ink well. Sarah cracked a grin and picked up the pen. When she found the next empty slot, she signed her name.

The man opened the door behind the curtain. "Enter at your own risk."

Sarah approached the door, greeted by a cacophony of conversations, clinking glasses, and surfer music on the jukebox in the corner. Behind the unassuming door within the odd-looking bookstore cover, there was an immersive tiki bar, complete with long tiki masks, torches with fake flames, and bamboo bar stools. There were multi-colored orbs on the ceiling and a glowing cave wall toward the back of the place that complemented the laminate stone flooring. She noticed that the bar off to the left was well-stocked, lined with the largest selection Sarah had ever seen.

And the place was hopping, even in the middle of the afternoon.

Behind the bar, a man with blond hair smiled, his eyes wide with excitement when he saw her.

"Sarah, long time, no see!" he said, waving at her frantically.

Sarah worked her way through a few people and found a spot at the end of the bar. "Hey, Teek. It's been forever."

It had been too long since she'd seen him last. She'd known Teek since he was a teenager, when she used to come visit her grandparents in the summer.

"Yeah, so what do you think of my new place?"

"It's neat. But what's up with the bookstore facade?" Sarah pointed her thumb toward the entrance on the other side of the curtain.

"Teek's Tiki Bar is the first speakeasy tiki bar in the

area, perhaps even the state. You remember those speakeasy places in the twenties, right?"

"Yeah."

"Totally like that, but a tiki bar hidden in the back instead of a twenties-style bar. But anyway, I'm so psyched to see you, Sarah," Teek said, leaving his spot behind the bar. She felt his muscles flex when he gave her a hug. "How's your pops?"

They ended their embrace and she smiled. "He's good. So, how are you? What have you been up to?"

"Oh, you know…just running the bar and catchin' waves whenever I can. Not so many goobers out there in the off-season, so it's a cinch to boogie on down the line and get in the pocket."

Sarah nodded, trying to wrap her head around his lingo. She knew "goobers" were annoying people, but couldn't remember what "boogie on down the line" or "in the pocket" meant, though she figured they had something to do with surfing.

"That's good, Teek."

"Yeah. And I've been hitting the weights." Teek flexed. His tanned biceps bulged, and her eyes widened faintly. "Gotta keep up my physique. And, plus, I've been working other areas for better balance and strength on the board."

"Oh?"

"Yeah, for longer rides, dude." Teek laughed. "Sorry, I meant 'dudette.'"

"So, Teek. Have you seen Mr. Montgomery lately?"

Teek scanned the crowd, making a show of shading his eyes as if he were looking out into sea in search of a "gnarly" wave.

"Nah," he said, "don't see that kook anywhere."

"How often does he come in here?"

"He's here later in the day, usually." Teek glanced at his watch. "Should be here in an hour, if I had to guess."

Sarah paused, thinking about what she should do for the next hour. Her stomach rumbled. "Okay, I'll stop back then." She'd decided that she'd stop by at the Crab Shack for some coconut shrimp. Her mouth watered at the thought.

"Don't you want a drink before you go? Maybe a Sandy Wave Margarita?"

Sarah crinkled her nose. "That sounds horrible."

"No way. It's a hit around here. It's orange juice with peach schnapps, but with a little fun twist."

Sarah could sense what the "little fun twist" was. "Whatever happened to just a Fuzzy Navel?"

Teek wore a mischievous smile. "I like to make my own creations."

"So, why is it called a Sandy Wave?"

"The extra addition dilutes the orange juice color and it looks more sandy than orange."

"And the wave part?"

Teek snickered. "Oh, you will feel the wave after only one sip!"

Sarah's eyes grew wide. Knowing Teek, you'd probably feel the crash of that wave later as well. No way she would be able endure that and keep her head straight. Teek liked to live on the edge, but Sarah was a bit less than a lightweight. "Well, I'd love to, but I have to get going."

"All right, Sarah." Teek gave her another hug. "So stoked to see you again."

"You too, Teek. I'll see you a little later." Sarah turned to make her way back through the crowd, but paused and said over her shoulder, "Do you serve mojitos?"

"Sure do!" Teek said with a smile.

"Maybe I'll have one of those when I get back."

Teek gave her a wink. "You got it, dudette."

Just then, someone flagged down Teek for another drink. He nodded at them and got back to work, mixing up a blue concoction for them. Sarah shook her head and smiled. He was always fun and energetic. One of the many things she liked about Teek.

Sarah exited the bar, turning to see Teek waving at her as she left.

alking along the boardwalk, Sarah saw Toby's Crab Shack. Her mind fixated on the coconut shrimp Toby had described when he stopped by Larry's Pawfect Boutique. Stomach growling, she opened the door to the Crab Shack and stepped inside.

The atmosphere was much different from the tiki bar next door, and as she scanned the restaurant, she realized why. The place was empty, except for a couple seated at the far right of the restaurant. With the boardwalk hopping, she wondered if people just weren't in the mood for crab and shrimp today.

She was greeted by a hostess and seated at a table for two. The hostess left a menu on the table, heading back toward her station at the front of the restaurant. Sarah

could see her cellphone lying face up on her podium—
she seemed to be playing some sort of game on the
phone while she waited for more patrons to walk in.

Sarah peered over at the only other table that was
occupied, then saw a man turn around and look at her,
face beaming.

"Sarah!" he said, then rushed over to her table.

"Hey, Toby."

Toby shot Sarah a bright smile. "Stopping by for
some coconut shrimp?" Toby said. He was wearing
khakis and a beige vest over an olive-green undershirt
and boots. He was a tall, brawny man and Sarah could
definitely see the fisherman in him.

"You better believe it. I'm stoked to try it." She shook
her head—already, Teek had rubbed off on her. "Very
excited to try it."

"Good, good. Coming right up! Anything to drink?"

"Iced tea."

"You got it."

When Toby left her table and zipped toward the back
of the restaurant, going through a doorway to what she
figured was the kitchen, Sarah pulled her phone out and
dialed Adam.

Adam picked up after a single ring.

"Hi," he said, his voice hushed.

"Hey, Adam."

"Give me a second. I need to get somewhere where I can talk." A few moments later, Adam's voice was louder: "So what did you find out?"

"I spoke with Cecil."

"Did he give you any new information?"

"Not really."

Adam sighed.

Sarah continued, "But the maid did."

"The maid? You mean, Janet? We questioned her, and she said she didn't hear or see anything."

"Right, I know. She didn't want to talk to the cops."

Adam huffed. "She can get in big trouble for withholding information."

"She has her reasons, Adam. Just listen: she heard Mr. and Mrs. Montgomery arguing the evening of the murder."

"So?"

"So, she heard Mr. Montgomery say he was going to kill Frederick Critsworth. Strangle him, to be exact."

"Okay…"

Sarah paused. "Okay?" What was he not getting? She couldn't have been more transparent.

"Sarah, you should know better than anyone that people say things they don't mean when they are heated. Remember what happened last time? Besides, the maid might have heard wrong."

"No, because I went to the Dolphin Motel and found Mrs. Montgomery there. She says that her husband did say that and that she doesn't know where he was the night of the murder."

Sarah waited for a response but was only met with silence. Maybe she really did need to spell everything out for him.

"Shouldn't you call this in, Adam?"

"No, we need something more concrete."

"Well," Sarah said, "I guess I could do some more digging. Use my secret ninja skills again when I talk to Mr. Montgomery."

More silence.

"What do you say, Adam?"

Adam's voice tensed. "I don't know, Sarah. This might be too dangerous. You'll really have to be—"

"Discreet. Adam, 'discreet' is my middle name."

Sarah reflected that she was more discreet without her cousin, Emma, around. Since she'd be going alone, she wouldn't have to worry about Emma being a loose cannon and saying something they'd both regret.

"Listen, Sarah. I don't want you to go alone..."

"I understand, but Mr. Montgomery is not going to talk to a cop. It's best if I go alone. I'll call right after I'm done. And besides, Teek will be there."

"Oh, yeah. Teek. I forgot about him."

Sarah chuckled. "Don't tell me you're still mad about that summer—"

"Oh, no. Teek's fine. He's great. Handsome, blond, and muscular—a regular Fabio. But, you know, he's not that bright."

Sarah shook her head. "He might not be the brightest, but he's kind, and more importantly, no one would ever think to mess with Teek…which means no one will mess with me."

"You're right. But call me as soon as you're done!"

"Totally, dude."

CHAPTER 10

Sarah said her goodbyes to Adam and slid her phone into her pocket. A few minutes later, Toby brought her coconut shrimp platter over to her table, and she stared, googly eyed. The array of fried jumbo shrimp, crusted with coconut, was surrounding three small bowls of different sauces. On another plate was a heaping serving of waffle fries tossed in what looked like Old Bay spices.

"So, the coconut shrimp is made with jumbo shrimp, tossed with extra-large coconut flakes, Panko, and our secret seasoning," Toby said. "Then deep-fried golden brown to perfection. The waffle fries are also made with our secret seasoning."

"What are all these sauces?"

"Ah, I forgot to ask what sauce you'd like and decided

to bring you a variety to try." Toby puffed up his chest with pride. "The first one is our house tartar sauce, handmade with mayonnaise and sweet relish, capers, lemon juice, and shallots."

Toby pointed to the pink sauce. "This is our Pink Miami Sauce which is made similar to our basic tartar, only it has more of a kick to it. We add some smoked paprika and chili sauce, which gives it that pink color. Though, the addition of spices makes this one of our top dipping sauces."

Sarah gave him a nod of approval. That sauce definitely looked really yummy, and she couldn't wait to try it.

"And the last one," Toby continued, "is our coconut ranch sauce, which is made with coconut mayonnaise, and Italian seasoning."

Sarah's eyes lit up. She had never heard of it but was incredibly curious about how it would taste.

"Wow. This all looks delicious," Sarah said. "I can't wait to dig in."

Toby smiled. "Enjoy."

He seemed very appreciative and it made Sarah wonder again why his restaurant was rather empty. Then, Sarah realized that the dinner rush wouldn't be for another hour yet.

"Oh, I will," Sarah said, unfolding her napkin and

placing it on her lap. She smelled the entree and couldn't wait to take her first bite.

Toby left the table, and she picked up one of the crispy, golden-brown shrimp and dipped it into the house sauce. The sauce had a smooth consistency to it, and she could tell as the sweet smell of it reached her nose that it was definitely freshly made. Sarah bit into the shrimp, making a crunch. The melody of flavors played in her mouth, and she took her time, chewing slowly to enjoy the amazing textures and spices.

"My goodness," she said, out loud. She quickly covered her mouth, realizing someone might have heard her. She glanced at the people on the other side of the restaurant to see if they had, but the man seemed to be enjoying crab legs, while his wife savored the popcorn shrimp.

Sarah returned to her meal, enjoying not only the shrimp and fries, but all three dipping sauces. She would definitely have to gather the family to come here for dinner soon. Though she knew that they would all argue over which sauce was the best, at this moment, she couldn't decide.

Toby returned to ask how her meal was.

"Toby," Sarah said, her mouth still full, "this is the best shrimp and variety of sauces I think I've ever had."

Toby grinned wide and nodded with approval at her,

like he already knew he made the best. Toby seemed a little overconfident, which came across as a bit arrogant to her, but on the other hand, didn't he have every reason to be? She wasn't lying when she said it was the best.

He reached over and clutched her glass, and she saw his forearms were thick and one had a tattoo of a rose with a dagger through it. She noticed his other arm had a tattoo of a harpoon.

"Refill?" he asked.

"Sure," she said. "Nice tattoo, by the way. Were you in the Navy?"

"My father was. How'd you know?"

She pointed to the tattoo of the rose and dagger. "Means loyalty, right?"

Toby smiled. "Yes, a sailor's loyalty and willingness to fight anything." He dropped his gaze to his tattoo. "You know, he used to take me whaling with him. He taught me everything I know about fishing. Then he got cancer. He fought it over and over. But, unfortunately, it won in the end. So I got this tattoo in his honor."

"I'm sorry to hear."

Toby regarded Sarah. "It's okay. It was a while ago now, and he left me this restaurant. I have a lot of fond memories of him here. He taught me everything I know," Toby smiled, "including how to make fantastic coconut shrimp."

Sarah smiled. "I think you did him proud."

After her meal, she paid the bill and left the Crab Shack, waving goodbye to Toby.

"Come back soon, Sarah!"

"I will."

It was close to dinnertime, and Sarah couldn't help but notice that Toby's restaurant was still void of patrons. She surveyed the room, but all she saw were the empty tables and the pictures that adorned the walls. In the picture closest to her table, she could see a man holding up a large fish. What a catch! She wondered if it was Toby in the picture, and figured it must have been.

She let out a long breath, remembering the taste of shrimp. People don't know what they're missing, she mused.

Back out on the boardwalk, she noticed the Ferris wheel churning off to her right, almost completely filled to capacity. Scanning her surroundings, she saw people whiz by on roller blades, people with sunglasses and hats, trying to block the rays of sun. She could see the kids still playing in the sand out beyond the boardwalk, waves crashing down not more than a few yards beyond. Soon, the sandcastles they built would be washed away by high tide, but for now, it was probably the last thing on their minds.

Stepping along, Sarah soon found herself outside Teek's. She swept through the tiny bookstore that served as a cover for the tiki bar within, and again, the bar area was still hopping.

Teek was too busy to notice her enter, but then, he pivoted and caught her in his view. He waved, then motioned toward a man Sarah figured was Mr. Montgomery. He was a large man, hunched over at the bar, gulping a glass of beer, his thick hands surrounding the glass as if he were strangling it.

Teek gave a thumbs up to Sarah, as if there'd been a plan and everything was going according to it. What a goof, she thought.

Mr. Montgomery was staring intently at his beer, unaware of Teek's gestures. Sarah found a spot next to the man and sat down. The man took one final swig of his beer, slamming the empty glass down onto the bar top.

The man's voice boomed, cutting through the sounds of chatter all around them. "Another one, Teek."

Teek glanced at Sarah as she got comfortable, and his gaze shifted to the man beside her. "Same thing, Mr. M.?"

"Yeah, keep 'em coming," the man said, motioning his hand like a wheel, round and round again.

Teek nodded, then regarded Sarah. "How about you, ma'am?"

"Yes, I'll have that drink now. And easy on the rum," Sarah said, as Teek took off down the other end of the bar to grab some glasses and ice. If there was one thing she knew about Teek, it was that he could have quite a heavy hand when it came to pouring alcohol. In fact, this poor chap next to her would probably hit his goal of pure oblivion if only he had ordered a mixed drink.

"You got it, dudette."

Sarah stifled a laugh and turned to see that Mr. Montgomery's expression was still sullen.

"Rough day?" Sarah asked the man.

"Rough year...Heck," the man said, not looking up from his empty glass, "rough life."

"Oh yeah?"

Mr. Montgomery glanced at Sarah. "You don't want to hear about my troubles, trust me," he said. Teek set a tall glass of dark beer in front of him, and he took a copious gulp, smacking his lips together. "This is my elixir. Solves all my problems."

"What problems?"

Mr. Montgomery chuckled, the first real emotion Sarah had witnessed the man express. "What problems?

Where do I even start? Maybe with my witch of a wife..."

Sarah noticed Teek deliver her the mojito, and nodded in appreciation, but quickly returned her gaze to Mr. Montgomery. "That's terrible," she said.

"It sure is. If I could do it all over again, I'd be more selective. Pick a woman who wouldn't wrong me in so many ways. But now I'm stuck..."

"How has she wronged you? If you don't mind me asking..."

"Don't mind at all—less I'll have to spend on therapy." He chuckled again. "Well, the latest escapade was this party we went to. We were in town for it, and I was looking forward to it. Trying to repair our marriage, you see? But just as things were looking up, she disappeared. Left the party early, around nine, if you can believe that. She calls me the villain, but she's the one who ditches me."

Teek was cleaning a glass nearby, and chimed in, "Bummer, dude."

"Indeed," Mr. Montgomery said. "'Bummer' is the right word for it."

"So where are you staying while in Cascade Cove?" Sarah asked.

"We were at the Beachside B&B, but now we're at the Dolphin. It's a bit of a dump compared to the B&B. And now I won't hear the end of that."

"You were moved because of what happened?"

Mr. Montgomery stopped mid-sip, taking a harsh gulp. He shot a look at Sarah. "You heard about that?"

"Yeah. Word travels fast around here. I even heard something else that I found interesting."

"What's that?"

Sarah hesitated, wondering how to phrase the thought that was swirling around in her mind. She knew she needed to be discreet, but the man was clearly drunk and perhaps he wouldn't mind the bluntness of her statement. She opened her lips, but before she could speak, he said, "What did you hear?"

Sarah took a sip of her mojito, noting the refreshing hints of lime and mint. It seemed that Teek had heeded her request. She cleared her throat. "I heard from someone I know that they overheard you say you would strangle Mr. Critsworth, the man who was found dead at the B&B."

Mr. Montgomery paused, like he was considering her words. Then, the corners of his mouth ticked up, and she noticed the hint of a smile on his face. "I might have said that. Can't say I feel sorry that he's dead," he said, downing the last of his beer. He slammed the glass down on the counter, and his gaze bore through Sarah. "But I didn't kill him, if that's what you think."

"Well, I didn't—"

Mr. Montgomery got up abruptly and tossed a bill on the counter, one hand on his stool in an attempt to steady himself. "Though, I wish I had."

Sarah sat shocked as the man stumbled away, and before she knew it, he was gone in the crowd of people, likely leaving the bar for the night.

Teek came over to Sarah, shaking his head. "Unfortunate, that man."

Sarah's brows furrowed, and she put an elbow on the bar. "Why do you say that?"

"You haven't heard?"

Sarah shook her head. Did he have information that she didn't? She leaned closer. "Heard what?"

The song on the jukebox ended and Sarah waited for Teek to reply. Someone off at the other end of the bar guffawed, and a woman shouted, "Put on 'Sweet Home Alabama'!"

Before the popular song could start, Teek said, "Well, rumor mill says that Mrs. M. was cheating on him with Frederick Critsworth."

"What?"

"That's what I heard," Teek said. "If it's true, she's such a goober."

"Who told you that?"

The jukebox roared back to life as Teek scratched the

stubble on his chin, then yelled above the music, "I forget who, but you know what they say about loose lips and all. And here at the bar, I'm around loose lips all day."

CHAPTER 11

The next morning, Sarah was out on the beach with Rugby and Winston. It was early and the beach was almost completely vacant. She felt the saltwater breeze caress her face, and she threw the Frisbee, running barefoot with the dogs. Rugby caught it in midair, which was impressive the first few times. What wasn't impressive was the fact that he kept taking off with the Frisbee and not giving it back.

"Rugby!" Sarah yelled as she ran after the yellow lab, who was frolicking through the sand. Winston stayed right by Sarah's side. It didn't take long for Winston to get used to the sand, but he still seemed to not know what to make of it.

As Sarah ran, leash in hand, Rugby stopped abruptly and peered back. He dropped the Frisbee. Sarah exhaled a sigh of relief and jogged closer to him. But something caught Rugby's eye, and he took off in the opposite direction, leaving the Frisbee behind.

Sarah yelled again as Rugby passed her in full speed. Sarah made a disgruntled sound of frustration. She glanced over her shoulder to see what he was after. There was a group of seagulls huddled around, looking for breakfast. As Rugby drew closer to them, the seagulls squawked and dispersed into an explosion of white feathers.

Rugby stopped again, looking around to see where they all had gone. He eyed Sarah, with his pink, floppy tongue hanging out the side of his mouth. He looked like he was grinning.

Sarah walked toward the Frisbee, which was only a few feet away, and picked it up. Rugby came charging back, leaping into the air, waiting for her to throw it once more.

"No way," Sarah said, shaking her head. "I'm not falling for that again." She grabbed Rugby's collar and snapped the leash on him. "C'mon, that's enough exercise for one day." She walked with them over to her sandals and slipped them on, then they made their way back to the boardwalk.

The mornings were serene on the boardwalk, since most of the people were either sleeping in, like her cousin, out for breakfast, or off sight-seeing at the light-house or another popular destination. There were still people out, though not as many as in the afternoon and early evening.

A carefree breeze cascaded through Sarah's hair, and she took in the smell of saltwater. Waves crashed off to her left as she headed south toward the Ferris wheel. It was motionless now, a contrast to the surrounding movement. Other early birds were walking. Some had dogs, and there was one person who was walking their cat. Sarah chuckled to herself at the sight. There were other people who were riding their bikes, apparently unable to restrain themselves from getting a jump on the day. Not a cloud was in the sky—it was the start of a perfect day for fun.

But Sarah wasn't in the mood for fun. Her mind churned as she walked.

She'd hoped taking the dogs to the beach would do her good and help her get her mind off of the murder. So far, it hadn't, and she was still unsure of what to think about what she'd learned the previous day.

She had tried to call Adam earlier, though she had to leave a voicemail, and he hadn't called back.

Now, all she could do was wait, and think.

It would make sense that Mr. Montgomery made a threat toward Critsworth if his wife was having an affair with the man—that is, if what Teek said last night was true. And if all three of them were at the party, and it was Mrs. Montgomery who had left early, it would make sense that she left *with* Frederick Critsworth. What if Mr. Montgomery saw her leaving with the man...

"Hmm," she said aloud. "That would certainly give him a motive to strangle him..."

Off to her right, she saw two familiar faces.

"Sarah!"

"Hi, Marigold. Charlotte," Sarah said, waving.

Marigold was wearing her huge, brimmed sun hat, with large glasses and ruby lipstick. Her strawberry-blonde curls hung loose, framing her face. Charlotte, always the more conservative type, wore a white sun dress with flats and her bleached hair was up in a casual but nice bun.

The women made small talk with Sarah, telling her about their newfound partnership in the vineyards. Apparently, all was going well with the business, and they were back up to peak production.

Then it finally dawned on Sarah. Charlotte and Marigold would probably be running with the same crowd as the Montgomerys. She was sure, if there was an upscale party, that Marigold and Charlotte would definitely have been there. "Say, did you two go to the mixer the other night?" Sarah asked.

"Of course, we did. We wouldn't miss that for the world," Marigold said. "What a fantastic time that was." Marigold glanced at Charlotte, who nodded in agreement.

Bingo! Sarah wasn't sure who was lying, Mr. or Mrs. Montgomery. Maybe they could help her. Sarah took a quick breath and asked what was on her mind: "Say, do you remember seeing Mrs. Montgomery there?"

"I believe so," Charlotte said, looking at Marigold.

Marigold mulled it over a moment. "Why, yes," she said, nodding. "Yes, she was. She was hanging around this fellow."

"Who?"

Marigold and Charlotte exchanged glances, probably hoping the other had an answer.

Sarah tried a different approach. "Was it Mr. Montgomery?"

"Oh, dear. I remember. It wasn't her husband, but I can't tell you who the man was." Marigold put her hand to her chest.

Sarah wasn't sure if she was appalled by the fact that Mrs. Montgomery was talking with another man that night, or that she couldn't place who the man was that was at the party with Mrs. Montgomery.

"He's an out-of-towner, I believe," Charlotte said.

Sarah felt confused, but the man who Mrs. Montgomery was with was not her problem. She needed to know who left the party first, and when. "Did you see Mrs. Montgomery leave?"

Marigold pressed her finger into her chin, thinking. "Now I'm sure it wasn't her husband, because I remember seeing him at the bar." Marigold seemed to still be stuck on whom the man was that was with Mrs. Montgomery.

"But when did she leave?"

Marigold fixed her gaze on Sarah. "That's the thing— I remember her leaving with that man. I don't know when exactly, but it was rather early, before the toast ceremony. I only remember because I bumped into Mr. Montgomery at the bar. And I thought it was quite odd that he was there when his wife walked out with the other man."

"Wait," Sarah said. "So, she left with the mystery man?"

CHAPTER 12

Sarah headed back toward where her grandpa's boutique was. Her pace had quickened by the new information she'd just obtained.

Along the way, she had to keep Rugby and Winston in line—they were intent on greeting everyone who came within ten feet of them. Even the seagulls that swooped nearby caught their attention and caused them to go wild.

"I need to get you two out more often," she muttered, coercing them toward the boutique.

Once there, she strode around the side of the boutique and uncoiled the short gardening hose to spray the dogs' feet to rid them of sand and dirt. She grabbed a towel she had left on the railing leading to the back door and dried the dogs paws before allowing them to enter the shop. The bell above the entrance of the boutique jingled above her head.

She let the dogs off their leashes, and they bounded into the boutique. Soon, she could hear them lapping up water from their bowls. Misty streaked by, dodging the canines. She purred lightly as she rubbed Sarah's legs, tickling her.

That's when she heard Emma's voice behind the register. She was speaking to Grandma.

"No, you just did a 'No Sale,'" Emma said.

"But the drawer opened and now I can put the money in the drawer."

"No, you can't."

"What do you mean, I can't?" Grandma said, putting a bill in the drawer. "I just did."

Emma took the money back out and closed the drawer. "No, you can't."

Grandma put her hands on her hips. "And why is that?"

Emma sighed. "Because, if you do a 'No Sale' it won't mark the item out of inventory. It will mess it all up."

"Bah, nonsense, dear. I'll just mark it in inventory manually. We can do that, can't we?"

Emma rubbed her temples, a sign that she was getting frustrated. "Technically, yes. But it's complicated. There're a lot more steps to it and you—"

Sarah cleared her throat.

Grandma looked up and smiled. "Hello there, Sarah," Grandma said. She ran a rag across the counter. "Where were you yesterday? You were gone quite a while, and didn't take the dogs with you."

"Bet she was on another date with Adam," Emma chimed in.

Sarah shook her head at her cousin and regarded her grandma. "I went to get coconut shrimp at the Crab Shack and stopped in at Teek's place."

"Teek?" Grandma and Emma said in unison.

"Yeah," Sarah said, and saw both of them giving her scandalous looks. "What?"

Grandma shrugged. "No reason, dear. Teek is a fine gentleman. Very sweet. Does Adam know?"

Sarah furrowed her brows. "Does Adam know what?"

"Nothing." Grandma continued her dusting. "So, how is Teek?"

"He's good."

"Oh? What all did he say?"

"Not much. Said he's been running the bar, lifting weights, and surfing."

"A bar?" Grandma pulled items off a shelf above her head and placed them on the counter she'd just dusted.

"Yeah," Sarah said. "Teek's Tiki Bar."

"Well, that sounds like fun. I'll have to stop in and say hello."

"But, Grandma," Sarah said, as a confused look washed across her face, "you don't drink."

Grandma planted her fists on her hips, still holding the rag. "Who says?"

"Well, I've never seen you drink."

"Then I guess you don't know me well enough." Grandma chuckled. She reached up to the now empty shelf and wiped her rag across it. A cloud of dust plumed above her head. She coughed and waved her hands. "You and your cousin need to get Lawrence to help you dust this place." She set the rag down behind the counter, and strolled out, clearing her throat. "I need to go up and get more water."

Sarah didn't realize how dusty it was up there. She also couldn't remember the last time they'd moved anything on that particular shelf. "Okay, Grandma," Sarah said.

Grandma walked toward the door, then turned around. "So, I was thinking, maybe we can bake a chocolate cake sometime. Your choice."

Emma nodded with enthusiasm.

"Yeah, I think that would be nice," Sarah said with a smile.

"Great. Let me know what you girls want, and I'll go shopping later for some ingredients."

Both girls nodded, and Grandma strode through the door to the upstairs apartment.

Once she was out of sight, Emma plopped herself down onto her stool and said, "So…what did Teek really say?"

Sarah told her cousin everything she'd learned so far. Emma sat there, absorbing every morsel. She told her what the maid had overheard about the threat, what Teek had said about Mrs. Montgomery having an affair with Critsworth, and the tidbits she'd learned from Marigold and Charlotte about Mrs. M. leaving the party early.

"Maybe it wasn't Mr. Montgomery who killed Critsworth," Emma said.

"But he told his wife he wanted to strangle him."

"You said Mrs. Montgomery left the party early with a man. And based on what Teek told you, it had to be Frederick Critsworth." Emma was leaning so far forward she was practically off her stool. "You should call Adam and tell him."

"You know Adam will say it's all hearsay."

Emma huffed. "Yeah, yeah. I can practically hear him say that. His favorite word."

Sarah chuckled. "He'll say we need something 'concrete.'"

"We'll get there. So, Mrs. Montgomery is our prime suspect."

"I don't know."

"Listen, she was the last to see Frederick Critsworth alive. The last one with him. She has to know something. Who else could it be?"

Emma was right. The woman was awful and manipulative—a liar and a cheat. Worst of all, she was an opportunist. She was also with him the last hour before his death. Everything seemed to add up. "You're right."

"So, what are you going to do?"

Sarah pressed her lips together, looking pensively at her cousin. "I have to find Mrs. Montgomery."

CHAPTER 13

*O*nce Grandma had come back down to the boutique, Sarah left to make her way to the Dolphin Motel. She couldn't wait to find the woman again—she had a lot of questions for her.

At the Dolphin Motel, she strolled to the front desk to inquire about which room the Montgomerys were staying in, and the hesitant clerk gave her the information she needed after little prodding. Telling them she was a friend had been enough to get the room number, apparently.

Sarah strode along, scanning the numbers on each room until she found room number Twenty-One.

"Here we go," she said, approaching the door. She steeled herself and rapped on it.

Footsteps from within quickly approached the door. "I'm coming," came a woman's voice.

The door sprang open and Mrs. Montgomery stood there, smiling at Sarah. She wore a silk robe and her hair was wrapped in a scarf, though Sarah noticed the woman's makeup was done. It was also the first time Sarah had gotten a good look at Mrs. Montgomery's eyes—two hazel gems accented with a bit too much eyeliner, and mascara that caused her lashes to clump together.

"Oh, Sarah. I wasn't expecting you," she said, adjusting her headscarf.

"Sorry, I just needed to talk to you about something."

Mrs. Montgomery paused, then said, "Well, I'm not proper yet."

"That's okay, it won't take too long." Sarah waited, unsure if the woman was going to let her in.

"Why, of course...come on in, Sarah." Mrs. Montgomery opened the door wider to allow Sarah to enter. "I was just getting ready to go out into the town."

"Oh?"

Mrs. Montgomery walked over to the vanity and sat down, undoing the scarf on her head. "They just opened up a new casino by the hotel and I've been dying to go there." She pulled the scarf off to reveal several large rollers underneath, and began to undo the rollers.

Peering at Sarah through the mirror, she smiled. "Can't resist the flashy lights and the sound of crashing coins. And who can say no to a cocktail?"

Sarah nodded.

"So, what is it you wanted to talk about?"

Sarah felt a wave of nervousness wash over her, though she was quick to squash it down. "I wanted to talk to you about the night of the mixer," she said, voice firm.

"Again?" Mrs. Montgomery huffed, undoing the last of the rollers and fluffing her hair with her fingers. She spun around and glared at Sarah. "I told you! My husband—"

"It's not about your husband," Sarah cut in. "It's about Frederick Critsworth."

Mrs. Montgomery's eyes got wide for a moment, like she'd seen a ghost.

Sarah continued, "I know you were with Frederick Critsworth the night of the mixer."

"Excuse me?"

"Everyone saw you. There were witnesses."

Mrs. Montgomery's face relaxed. She returned her gaze to the mirror again and grabbed a brush, brushing the curls back to loosen them. "Yes, so what if I was?"

"Well, you left the mixer with Mr. Critsworth, early, before the toast."

"Those things bore me."

"Admit it."

"Admit what? The fact that I was having fun, for once?"

"Don't you think it's quite odd that after you both left the mixer, Critsworth winds up dead?"

Mrs. Montgomery's face turned bright red. "Are you insinuating that I murdered Frederick?"

Sarah took a step closer to the woman. "Who else would have done it? You were the last one to see him, and you were the last one with him."

Mrs. Montgomery spun back around to face Sarah, the woman's stare boring into her. "Tell me, Ms. Shores, what exactly would I gain from killing the man?"

Sarah stared at her, unsure of how to answer the question.

Mrs. Montgomery continued, "Money? He's better alive to me than dead."

Sarah was speechless.

"If you need to know the truth, Ms. Shores, then here it is: Yes, I was planning a nightcap with him after the party, but plans change. We got back to the B&B and we went to our separate rooms. I told him I was going to slip into something a little more comfortable. I was reapplying my makeup when I heard the sirens. When I came out of my room to see what the fuss was about, the police were already in the Sea Breeze Room. I went back into my room and locked the door. For all I know, it could have been my husband. I told him that night that I was going back to the B&B with Frederick. For all I know, he followed us, and when I went into my room, he followed Frederick into his and killed him."

Sarah's eyes went wide. How could she say such a thing?!

Before Sarah could reply, Mrs. Montgomery whipped back toward the mirror and said, "Now, if you don't mind, I'd like you to leave before I call the police on you for trespassing."

"I'm not trespassing."

Mrs. Montgomery slammed the brush down. "Then I'll call them for harassment and stalking! Now get out, now!"

CHAPTER 14

Sarah drove back to the boutique feeling slightly defeated. The conversation with Mrs. Montgomery didn't go the way she had expected. But how did she expect it to go? What was she thinking, accusing Mrs. Montgomery of a murder when she didn't have a good motive to back it up? Emma had really gotten to her, but it wasn't Emma's fault. She had made the decision to go to the Dolphin Motel and accuse a woman of murder. She couldn't do something like that again. Not if she wanted to find the culprit who ended a man's life.

She pulled up to the boutique and let out a long breath. She was back where she started. Taking the key out of the ignition, she slid out of the car. She wasn't sure how she was going to tell Emma what had happened.

As she walked up to the boutique, she saw Emma and Grandma coming out of the front door with the dogs. Emma turned and waved.

"Sarah," she called out, smiling. "We were just about to leave a note on the door for you to let you know we are taking the dogs for a walk."

Sarah walked up to them, taking Rugby's leash from Emma. "I'll go with you. I need a walk, myself."

Emma leaned in closer to Sarah so Grandma couldn't hear. "So, was it Mrs. Montgomery?"

Sarah shook her head. "I'll tell you what happened later."

"C'mon, girls. Let's go enjoy what's left of this beautiful day." Grandma stood there waiting, Winston sitting by her feet. She liked walking Winston, since he was calm and listened to her commands. Rugby, on the other hand, tended to walk Grandma, and she was never up to being dragged by an eighty-pound, blond bundle of energy and mayhem.

They started walking on the main strip, when Sarah's stomach growled. "Oh boy," she said, holding her stomach. She couldn't remember the last time she had eaten.

"You hungry, dear?" Grandma asked.

"Yeah, I guess I am."

"Me too," Grandma said. "Maybe we could try that new place Grandpa was talking about. It's that sushi place that just opened on the boardwalk. Oh, what's it called?"

Emma raised an eyebrow at Grandma. "The Board Wok?" Emma asked.

"That's it. The Board Wok." Grandma chuckled. "Isn't the name cute?"

Sarah and Emma both nodded and burst into laughter.

They turned and made their way to the boardwalk. Soon they were walking up to the hole-in-the-wall place.

A few people were sitting at tables outside the sushi bar, and Sarah tried to herd the dogs around them as they stepped toward the front of the eatery. There was an outside bar area, where her grandma was now standing.

Sarah sidled up to Grandma and saw a man behind the counter. "Hello," he said.

Sarah, Emma, and Grandma said their hellos. The man introduced himself as Yuki Fujimoto. He smiled and some wrinkles appeared on his face, though he didn't appear to be any older than fifty. He was thin, with black hair, and his white jacket was spotless. Yuki noticed the dogs and smiled. "Well, look at that. Two beautiful dogs. What are your names?"

"Rugby and Winston," Sarah said. Both dogs sat next to each other, panting and looking up at the man.

Yuki clapped his hands. "They are handsome." He looked up at Sarah, Emma, and Grandma. "I have a dog too. A poodle."

Sarah smiled. She loved poodles. "What's his name?"

"Ralph. He's a good dog. Very handsome, like yours. So, what can I do for you?"

"First off, we'd like to welcome you to the neighborhood," Grandma said.

"Thank you," Yuki said. "Do you live around here?"

"We have the pet boutique down that way," she said, motioning to one side.

"Oh, how nice. Say, do you sell bandanas? Every time I get him back from the groomer, he gets a new bandana —it's something they do every time. Saint Patty's Day, he got a green one. Around Valentine's Day, he got one with hearts on it. He seems to like them, and I want to see about getting him a whole collection."

"Yes," Sarah said, "we have a lot of bandanas, and we also switch up the themes and colors for the seasons and holidays. We also sell bow ties and sweaters."

Yuki's eyes lit up. "You have bow ties and sweaters,

too? I'll have to check it out. See, Ralph is a very stylish dog."

"Sounds good."

"So, what will you have?"

Grandma squinted, studying the board behind Yuki. "I think we are in the mood for some rolls." Grandma glanced at both Emma and Sarah to gauge their preference. They nodded in agreement.

Emma was the first to order. She wasn't a fan of sushi, but she loved rolls. She got the peanut avocado roll drizzled with a Thai peanut sauce, and then asked about the crispy sweet potato roll.

Yuki explained it was a roll stuffed with pieces of sweet potato that was deep-fried and tossed in a brown sauce.

Emma licked her lips. "Yeah, I'll have that, too."

Grandma decided on the tuna rolls and an order of the California rolls. She wasn't one to experiment. She liked what she liked, and that was that. Unless it was a sweet. That was a different game altogether.

Sarah eyed up the crunchy crab rolls covered with a garlic cream sauce. There was also a spicy tuna roll with cucumber, tempura flakes, and avocado, with a spicy mayo sauce. She wasn't able to decide which she wanted more, so she ended up getting both.

They paid for their order and said their goodbyes.

They found a seat alongside the boardwalk, and Rugby and Winston lay in a shaded spot near the table, both panting. Emma reached into her backpack and pulled out a portable water dish, then poured water from a bottle that was also in her pack. The dogs took turns lapping up the water, then lay on the ground, satiated.

Sarah noticed her grandma was struggling to get her chopsticks from their paper wrapper. "Need help?"

"No, I'm fine." After another few seconds of struggling, Grandma was successful at unwrapping the chopsticks. She pulled them out and stared at them with trepidation.

"You've never used chopsticks before, Grandma?" Emma asked.

"Sure, I have, sweetie," Grandma said, breaking them apart. She fumbled with them for a moment, then got her grip on them.

"I'm sure Mr. Fujimoto would give you a fork if you asked," Sarah said. "Want me to go up and get one?"

"Bah." Grandma swatted the air with one hand as she held both chopsticks in the other. She shakily lowered them, trying to snatch a sushi roll. After a few attempts, she was able to get a grip on one and pull it away from the group of six.

Grandma's hand quaked as she guided the roll up toward her mouth, but a moment before her maneuver was successful, the roll slipped from between her chopsticks, bounced on the tabletop, and cascaded through the air. Before hitting the ground, Rugby's mouth opened, and he gobbled up the sushi roll in one fell swoop.

Sarah's eyes grew wide. "Rugby!"

Rugby blinked twice, then lapped up more water before laying back down. He remained alert, likely hoping another roll would find its way into his mouth.

"I'll get you a fork," Emma said. She left the table and headed back up to where Yuki Fujimoto was preparing someone else's order.

Emma was back as quickly as she left, and Grandma took the fork from her with an appreciative nod. "Thanks, dear."

Grandma speared a sushi roll with her fork and raised it to her mouth. This time, she was able to enjoy it. "Mmm," she said, chewing slowly. "This is amazing. I have a feeling Yuki will be here for a while."

After enjoying their sushi, they continued along on the boardwalk until Grandma ran into some old friends and began talking.

Emma turned to Sarah. "So, what happened with Mrs. Montgomery?"

"It wasn't her."

Emma gave Sarah a confused look.

Sarah continued, "She has no motive."

There was a brief silence and Sarah could hear the chatter of people around them, the waves crashing, and the seagulls squawking as she waited for Emma to respond. When she didn't, she added, "Think about it. She couldn't be doing it for money. If that were the case, he was better off alive than dead to her." She realized she was parroting Mrs. Montgomery, but it was the truth.

"But she was the last person seen with him before he died."

"True, and Mrs. Montgomery admits that she was about to have a nightcap with Mr. Critsworth, but when they got back to the B&B, she strode into her room to freshen up. By the time she was done, the police were already there."

"As Adam would say, 'That's hearsay,'" Emma said. "Of course, she's going to say she had nothing to do with his death."

Sarah shook her head. "There's about twenty minutes unaccounted for. Anything could have happened."

"Are you thinking it was Mr. Montgomery, then?"

"I don't know." Sarah mulled it over for a moment. Then an idea struck her. "But I think I know how I can find out for sure."

CHAPTER 15

Sarah made her way down the boardwalk, heading south. She walked like she was on a mission. Emma stayed behind, waiting for Grandma to finish chatting, so she could take her back home with the dogs. Sarah was grateful that her cousin was willing to take care of everything while she ran this one, secretive errand. But then again, Emma was dying to know what Sarah would find.

When she saw the sign for Teek's, she entered, seeing the same man dressed in '20s attire as before.

There, resting on the table the man was seated behind, she noticed the guest book.

"Hello there, madam," he said with a smile. "Back so soon?"

BETRAYAL AT THE B&B

Sarah pointed down at the guestbook. "Does everyone who comes in here sign this?"

The man's demeanor changed to match the seriousness of Sarah. He gave her a quizzical look. "Yes, mostly. I ask everyone to sign before they go in, but you don't have to if you really don't want to. Teek just likes to have it as memorabilia."

"May I look at it?"

The man paused, then shrugged. "I guess. It's just a guestbook."

She paged back in the book. "Are these dates accurate?"

"Why, yes. Wouldn't make much sense if they weren't."

Sarah looked up at the man and nodded, smiling. When she found the date she was looking for, she slid her index finger down the page as she scanned the names. Then, her finger stopped when she spotted the name: "Montgomery."

Sliding her finger to the left, she saw that he was at Teek's place the night of the murder. She flipped to a page the night after and found the Montgomery name again. It was the same handwriting. The same lazy loop before the "M" in "Montgomery."

Sarah pointed at the door, motioning to go into the bar. "May I?"

The man reached over and flipped the pages of the guestbook to the current date and time. "If you don't mind signing the guestbook."

Sarah smiled. "Of course." She picked up the feathered pen and dipped it in the inkwell. She scratched her name in the box below the last signature. When she was done, the man pulled back the curtain and opened the door.

Sarah hurried into the tiki bar and scanned for an open spot at the crowded bar. Teek spotted her and waved her over, pointing to a seat near the end of the bar. People were talking loudly and laughing as she made her way through the crowd. When she reached the bar, she hopped up on the stool, facing Teek.

"What's happening, dudette?" Teek asked, smiling. "Glad you came back."

"Yeah." Sarah glanced around. "This place seems to always be hopping."

Teek grinned. "I love what I do. You know what they say, 'happy bartender, happy bar!'" Teek picked up a glass from under the bar and wiped the inside with a towel, drying it. "Would you like a mojito?"

Sarah was slightly impressed that he remembered her drink. With all the patrons in and out every day, she'd assumed he wouldn't remember.

"No, thanks," she said. "I came here because I wanted to ask, does Mr. Montgomery usually leave early?"

"Hmm, now that I think of it, when he's in town, he always stays till we close at two in the morning. Dude's got some killer stories. The only time he left early was when you were here. Total buzzkill."

Sarah ignored his slight jab toward her. "Was he here last Saturday night?"

Teek scratched his chin. "Yeah, as a matter of fact. I remember because that was the night he came real early. I think sometime around nine o'clock, and he was in a penguin suit, already half wasted."

"You mean a tuxedo?"

"Yeah, what a night that was. I felt like a babysitter. Now, that night, he was the total buzzkill. Thought I would have to go to extreme measures just to get him home. But he eventually got up on his own and was able to walk."

"So, he was here until closing?"

"Sure was," Teek said. "No doubt."

"Thanks," Sarah said, rushing away from the bar.

"Wait," Teek called after her, his hands out at either side. A beer glass was still in his left hand and the towel in his right. "No drink?"

"Not tonight," Sarah called back. "But I'll be back soon to catch up. Thanks!"

Sarah headed back to the apartment. She had all the proof she needed, but if it wasn't Mr. Montgomery and it wasn't Mrs. Montgomery, who could it be? She felt she was just as stuck as the police. There were no more clues, no motives, and no opportunities.

Once inside, she saw Emma laying on the couch.

"Em," Sarah said as she walked into the apartment.

"What?"

"Mr. Montgomery didn't do it."

"What do you mean?" Emma asked, sitting up and staring at Sarah.

"I went back to Teek's, and it turns out that Mr. Montgomery was there the night of Critsworth's murder."

"Maybe he went and killed the guy after he left the bar."

"No way. Mrs. Montgomery left the party around eight p.m. with Mr. Critsworth. Charlotte and Marigold said they saw Mr. Montgomery at the open bar after his wife left. And I just finished talking to Teek, who said that Mr. Montgomery was at his bar sometime around nine p.m. still in his tux, already half wasted. I assume from drinking at the mixer."

Emma ran her hand through her hair, thinking.

"You're right. There's no way that he could leave the mixer, go to the B&B and strangle Mr. Critsworth, then make it back to Teek's Tiki bar in that short amount of time." Emma sighed. "So, now what?"

"I don't know, but our only suspect has a solid alibi."

"We'll figure this out."

"I hope so," Sarah said. "But at this rate, we have nothing new to bring to the table. We are back where we started."

The next morning, Sarah was sitting at the dining room table, cutting and pasting. She had no leads, and she had decided that she should spend some personal time with Grandma before she set out for another cruise. In that time, Grandma was trying to catch up on one of her favorite hobbies. Apparently, she was behind over a year of supposedly important events to chronicle. And Sarah was most obliged to help. At least, that's what she figured. Sarah looked over at her grandma, a huge stack of newspapers off to one side.

"Go through these newspapers," Grandma instructed Sarah, "and find anything having to do with your grandpa, the boutique, or anything notable about any of the residents of the Cove."

"All these?" Sarah asked, eyeing the stack of papers.

"You said you'd help."

Sarah shifted her gaze to Emma, who was now laying back on the couch, a new whodunit novel in hand. "Em, are you sure you don't want to help, too?"

Emma didn't say a word, apparently engrossed in her novel.

"Don't worry," Grandma said. "She'll help me later, she just doesn't know it yet."

Sarah chuckled and grabbed a newspaper, paging through it.

"'Gerkins's Attempted Comeback an Epic Flop,'" Sarah read aloud. "And something about a Kate Thompson...not sure who this is."

"Not sure who that is either, but clip it out," Grandma said.

Sarah did as she was told. She scanned the rest of the newspaper, looking for other articles to clip.

"Nothing else noteworthy in this one," she said, setting it aside once she'd scanned every page.

"Keep going," Grandma said. "There's bound to be some gems in there."

"If you say so." Sarah picked up another newspaper, paging through it quickly. "Nothing in this one either, except Mr. Fudderman winning yet another bake-off."

"Clip it out. I have the perfect spot for it here, so glue it up while you're at it."

Sarah took scissors and clipped the Fudderman article. She flipped the page over, grabbed the glue stick, and made a square of glue on the back of the page. She handed the cut-out piece of newsprint to her grandma.

"Keep it up," Grandma said. "Get more gems like this one. Remember, this is a marathon, not a sprint."

Sarah squelched a groan, grabbing another paper. She paged through it and stopped when she caught a glimpse of her grandpa. Sarah smiled at the sight.

"I didn't know Grandpa built sandcastles."

"Oh, that was for the Sandcastle Competition last year."

"How did I miss this?"

"It was a week before you usually come to visit. He won first place, you know. Beat out the Thompson Twins and everything."

"Aren't the Thompson Twins *eight*?"

"Yeah, but for eight-year-olds, they build a mean sandcastle. Your grandpa trounced them, though. You should be proud."

Sarah cracked a smile. "What can Grandpa *not* do?"

"Dust the boutique, for one…and keep the kitchen from erupting in flames…"

Sarah shot her grandma a glance. "Good point."

"Glue that one, too," Grandma said. "I have a spot right here for it."

Sarah cut the article about the competition her grandpa had won the previous year, still shaking her head. She was learning more and more about her grandpa by the day.

Once cut out, she flipped the newspaper over, so she could glue the back, and froze.

"What's the matter?" Grandma asked.

Sarah sat, shocked, still looking at the newspaper.

"Emma," Sarah called.

Emma ignored her.

"Emma, you need to see this."

This time, Emma swung her legs and plopped her feet down on the floor. She placed a bookmark in her mystery novel and set it down gently on the coffee table. "This better be good," she mumbled, sauntering over to where Sarah was seated. "What is it?"

"Take a look."

Emma was breathing down Sarah's neck as they both stared at the article.

"Em, I think we found our next suspect."

CHAPTER 16

Sarah stared at the newspaper article. "The Banana Hammock: Less Than Savory."

Emma leaned over Sarah's shoulder. "What is it?"

"A Critsworth review of the Banana Hammock. It's from last year. Though, it's a mini preview."

"What's that?"

"Well, it looks like he reviews a restaurant in the area for a full review. Then, a second one as a preview that he will do a full review on the following year."

"So, you mean to say that Critsworth was back to review the Banana Hammock this year?"

"Looks like it."

Emma's eyes went wide. "What does it say?"

"'The Banana Hammock is unexceptional and ordinary. Everything is mediocre at best, including the decor. The food lacks any substance and is uninspiring. Though their top burger, the Hammock Burger with Boardwalk fries, wasn't terrible, it wasn't memorable either. They simply brought nothing new to the table.'"

Emma gave a pained expression. "Grandpa Larry would be hurt by this review. He loves the Banana Hammock."

Grandma looked up from her scrapbook. "We all do, and no miserable, old food critic can write a review to change that. Bad or good."

"There's more," Sarah said. "'Despite this, the restaurant is reliably packed. But you'd better have something in the fridge at home, because the likelihood of your joining the Clean Plate Club here is about as good as winning the lottery.'"

Emma and Sarah exchanged glances. "That's not very good," Emma said.

Sarah continued reading: "'I will be stopping by next year to try it again. Hopefully they will up their flavor and give me something that bites back, if only a little.'"

"It's not terrible. I've read worse."

"But it's not good, either."

"Do you think that Gary is capable of murder?"

"I doubt Kacey or her father would strangle a man over a less-than-savory review."

"You never know," Emma said. "If someone wrote

something negative about the boutique, I'd probably strangle them too. Think about it...it's their livelihood..."

"Yeah. I guess Kacey or her father would have the motive after this monstrosity, though I still doubt they did it."

"How could they not? A year after this, Critsworth is back in town..." Emma started.

"They knew he was going to write a follow-up and maybe they took care of him before he could touch pen to paper."

"You two are out of your minds," Grandma chimed in. "Those two are sweethearts."

"You think everyone's a 'sweetheart,' Grandma," Emma said, and returned her gaze to Sarah. "Listen, Sarah. Why don't you go over to the Banana Hammock and talk to Kacey, or better yet, her dad?"

"Her dad's out on that trip with Grandpa," Sarah said.

"Oh no! Do you think he'll try anything with Grandpa?"

"That's crazy, Emma," Grandma said. "Gary didn't kill anyone. You are both nuts."

"You better go talk to Kacey," Emma said to Sarah. "You know her better than all of us. She'll talk to you."

Sarah shrugged. "I guess it wouldn't hurt to talk to her. But I'm with Grandma on this—I can't imagine the

Hammocks could do anything like that. Plus, we don't have anything concrete enough..."

Sarah put the cap on the glue stick and folded the review, putting the paper in her pocket.

"Concrete enough? I think you're the one who's crazy," Emma said. "Just go over and see what you can find out. I'll take over for you at the scrapbooking station, here."

Sarah got up and put her sneakers on. "This shouldn't take too long," she said, and headed out of the apartment.

She reached the Banana Hammock and saw that the parking lot was half-full. At this time of the day, she knew the place should've been busier. Perhaps Critsworth had indeed had a chance to publish his follow-up review...

Once inside, she noticed that Kacey wasn't at her hostess station. Flo rushed by, and Sarah flagged her down.

"Is Kacey here?"

Before Flo could reply, Kacey came out and said, "Sarah, what's up?"

Flo scurried away as Sarah pulled the article from

her pocket. "I was just wondering about something. I found this article..."

Sarah handed the article and watched as Kacey read it. "Oh, this," Kacey said. "Yeah, this was the review Critsworth gave us last year. What about it?"

"Is this the first review he gave you like this?"

"Yeah. He'd never reviewed us before, and we were nervous when we found out he was coming in last year. You know his reputation..."

Sarah nodded.

Kacey handed the article back to Sarah and continued, "Anyway, what is this all about, Sarah?"

"I'm assuming you heard what happened to Frederick Crits—"

Just then, a tray of beverages spilled nearby, and Sarah looked up to see Flo scrambling to the ground in an attempt to clean up her mess. Kacey crouched to help Flo, and Sarah's mouth dropped when she spotted the logo on the bottom of Kacey's shoe.

Sarah's mind spun, and she remembered the picture Adam had shown her. The one of the logo that appeared to be some sort of animal. Could it be the same print? Then it dawned on her: she had taken a snapshot of the picture in Critsworth's file of that same shoe print with her phone. She scrambled for her phone and pulled up the picture.

Sarah gasped. It was the exact same logo.

After helping Flo clean up the mess, Kacey fixed her attention back on Sarah, who slid her phone into her pocket.

"So, you were saying?" Kacey asked.

"Yeah, were you at the B&B recently?"

Kacey's shocked look was quickly corrected. "No, I haven't been there in ages. Why?"

"Nothing," Sarah said, pocketing the article. "Say, I took up enough of your time. I should let you go."

Kacey gave a confused look as Sarah hurried toward the door. Once outside, she took out her cellphone. The screen came to life and the picture of the logo came back into view.

Her eyes went wide. It couldn't be...

She tapped the green "phone" icon on her cell and called Adam.

When he picked up, she could hear a man in the background yelling. "Let me out of here. It's not my fault! Those games are rigged!"

Then she could hear Adam's muffled voice. "Sir, if you don't keep it down, I'll have to transfer you to the cell in the other room."

Adam's voice was clear again: "Hello?"

Sarah realized that he must be working late. "Hey, what's going on?"

Adam huffed. "You know those ring toss games?"

"Yeah."

"Someone decided to take matters into their own hands when they didn't win."

"Well, I don't think he's wrong. They are rigged."

"That may be so, but when he lost, he hopped the counter and stole a stuffed bunny. Took off running. Chased him for about fifteen minutes all around the amusement park area. If you ask me, we just have a sore loser on our hands."

Sarah chuckled but quickly remembered why she had called him. "So, I think I might have a suspect."

"Oh?"

"Remember that picture of the shoe prints outside the B&B?"

"Sarah, I told you that those shoe prints could have been there at any time. It's just protocol for us to take pictures around the perimeter."

"I know, but it could narrow down the search."

"You're right. But it could have been someone who was inside the B&B all day. And there's so many foot-prints overlapping others. It's really hard to distinguish them, let alone focus on a specific shoe design."

"But hear me out," Sarah said. "I found a specific design. One with a bear logo."

"Yes, I remember that one. It's a partial footprint. We

won't be able to even match size. This isn't 'Forensics' on TV."

"I think it might be Kacey Hammock's. You know, at the Banana Hammock?"

Adam sighed. "Have you talked to her?"

"Yes, I just finished speaking with her."

"And what did she say?"

"She said she hasn't been to Cecil's B&B."

"Then there you go."

Sarah shook her head. "She could easily be lying."

"Sarah, I think you're jumping the gun here. First off, Kacey would never do something like that. We all know her."

Sarah could practically hear Emma say, "But how well do we know anyone?"

"And," Adam continued, "how many people do you think may have the same brand of shoe?"

Sarah heard some banging in the background and then the other man's voice: "I said, let me out of here!"

"I'm not kidding. If you don't keep quiet, I will put you in the isolated cell in the other room. So put a sock in it."

"How long are you going to keep him?"

"We'll hold him for a few hours and let him go when he calms down. Maybe overnight."

"Do you think it's necessary? Shouldn't you let the small fish go and focus on the big fish?"

"If we don't, then everyone will be stealing stuffed bunnies and running amok."

Sarah chuckled. "I guess you make a point."

"Listen, Sarah, maybe you should relax. I shouldn't have asked you to get involved. You're here to be with your family, and your grandmother is only in town for a few more days. Go spend some time with her. If we can't find anything substantial in that time, then you can help if you want."

He was right. Maybe she was jumping the gun, but she didn't want to take a break. Not when she felt like she was getting so close. On the other hand, she didn't want to make a fool of herself again, like she had with Mrs. Montgomery. She'd been too hasty in accusing her. Maybe she was too wrapped up in this and wasn't thinking clearly.

"Okay," she said, "I'll take some time—"

She was interrupted by another bang and heard the man's voice on the line. "You know, I have family too!"

"That's it!" Adam said. "Sorry, Sarah, I've got to go."

Adam really had his hands full with this guy, Sarah thought. But before she could say "bye," the call ended.

CHAPTER 17

The next morning, Sarah was in the kitchen with Grandma. They both had their aprons on, and they were already spotted with flour. There was an array of different-sized bowls with the exact measurement of each ingredient. Grandma, being a pastry chef on the Cascadian Cruise Line, always liked to be prepared before starting any dessert.

"Now," Grandma said. "There are a few things you should remember when baking a cake, that will keep it fluffy and moist."

Sarah wasn't much of a baker herself, but had fond memories of her childhood, standing on a chair and helping Grandma mix a bowl of frosting, or sitting on the counter and licking her chocolate-covered fingers.

Now, she was excited to actually learn how to bake a perfect triple-layer chocolate strawberry cake.

"First, always use real butter." Grandma picked up the small bowl with the butter in it and plopped it into the mixing bowl. "Margarine and butter substitutes contain more water than fat, and the fat in the butter will not only hold the cake together better but will also make it moist."

Sarah nodded. She had always assumed using real butter would make the cake better, but she never knew why.

Grandma picked up the bowl of eggs. "Now, we are going to put the egg in. But for one of these eggs"—Grandma picked up one egg and cracked it on the side of the counter—"we are going to separate the white from the yolk."

Sarah cocked her head. "Why just one?"

"We only need to do it to one, dear," Grandma said. "See, the white acts as a drying agent. We still need the whites, but taking one of them out helps keep moisture in the cake."

Sarah was still confused as to how this worked. She had never been good at chemistry, and trying to wrap her head around it might give her too much of a headache. She decided to just take Grandma's word for it.

Grandma continued going through each ingredient in detail. What they needed, how much they needed, and why. And Grandma really had a reason for everything. It was like a mathematical formula that made Sarah's mind spin. But she enjoyed combining all the ingredients, mixing everything together.

"We don't want to over-mix it, dear," Grandma said, leaning over Sarah.

"You can over-mix something?"

Grandma's eyes went wide. "Why, yes, it could make the cake dense and hard." She smiled. "But you're doing fine. I'll go get the pans greased and ready."

Just then, Emma walked in and opened the door to the refrigerator. Pulling out the orange juice, she poured herself a glass. She looked fresh, like she had just gotten out of the shower. She hopped up on the counter next to Sarah, who was still mixing the cake batter.

"Don't over-mix it," Emma said, taking another sip of her orange juice.

"I'm not," Sarah said, realizing she sounded like a child.

"Didn't Grandma make you do the alternating flour, milk technique?"

Sarah nodded. "And who are you to try to give me advice on baking?"

Emma's mouth dropped. "Are you insinuating that I'm a bad baker?"

Grandma walked over with two of the three pans, already greased. "Girls, no fighting in the kitchen. And Emma, don't you have a store to run?"

"Yeah," Emma hopped down from the counter. "Gotta start opening up in about ten minutes." She started walking toward the door. "Let me know when you make the chocolate cream cheese buttercream icing. I want to give it a taste test when it's done," she said over her shoulder.

Grandma shook her head. "I don't know what to do with that girl," she said and chuckled. She grabbed the third pan and placed it with the other two next to Sarah. "Okay, let's get this into the pans."

They started pouring, and after the pans were filled, Grandma placed them in the oven and set a timer. "I'm so glad you decided to help me bake this cake today. I was surprised when you asked."

"Yeah, I just need a break and I wanted to spend some more time with you before you left for another cruise."

Grandma nodded. "I understand. How's everything going with Adam and the investigation?"

"I seem to be just as stuck as they are."

"I see." Grandma gathered all the bowls, placing them in the sink to rinse. "Did you talk to Kacey yesterday?"

"Yeah, she said she hasn't been to the B&B. And I talked to Adam about a partial shoe print that has a logo of a bear on it, which seems to match a pair of shoes that Kacey has. But he said that it could mean nothing if others have the same shoe brand."

Grandma looked up. "Really? Can I see it?" She wiped her hands on a dish towel to dry them.

Sarah pulled out her phone and showed Grandma the picture of the shoe print. Grandma loved fashion and was usually up on the latest trends.

Grandma scrunched her face. "It does look like a woman's shoe, but I don't think I've ever seen that logo before."

Sarah stopped, her mind churning. Adam was right that it would be difficult to track down a person by their shoe if it was the same brand of shoe that many people wore. But what if it wasn't? What if this particular shoe was not as popular?

"Grandma, can you excuse me a moment?"

"Sure, Sarah, but be back soon. We still have to work on the icing."

Sarah rushed toward the doorway. "Okay, Grandma, I'll be right back."

Sarah made her way down the hall, almost bumping

right into Emma in her haste. When she made it to her room, she found her laptop and opened it, taking a seat on the bed.

"Sarah," came Emma's voice, and moments later she was standing in the threshold. "You almost hit me."

Sarah ignored her, opening her internet browser, which auto-loaded to her favorite search engine.

She typed in, "Shoe with bear logo."

In the search results, a polar bear logo came up.

Sarah muttered, "These shoes aren't even available in the U.S."

"What?" Emma asked. "Did you hear me?"

"Hold on." Sarah clicked on the logo. "Oh, wow."

"Tell me what's going on, Sarah." Emma walked over and plopped down next to Sarah on the bed.

"The logo is from a Norwegian brand of shoe."

"What logo?"

Sarah filled Emma in on the photo she'd seen of the footprint found at the B&B and how it resembled the logo on the bottom of Kacey's shoe. She grabbed her phone and showed her the picture she'd snapped of it at Adam's place.

"Is that a picture of a picture?" Emma asked.

"Yeah. It's a photo of that footprint, taken at the crime scene."

"And Kacey said she wasn't at the B&B?"

"She told me that, but I think she's lying. These shoes aren't what I'd call popular—they're only sold in Norway. They're from an island called 'Bear Island.'"

"What's 'Bear Island'?"

"I don't know. I've never heard of it."

Sarah searched for the term "Norwegian country polar bears."

"This is interesting," Sarah said.

Emma craned her neck to see the screen. She read aloud, "'A small island south of Norway, Bear Island was founded by Dutch explorers on June 10th, 1596.' Wow, that was a long time ago."

Sarah continued reading where Emma left off: "'It was named after a polar bear that was seen swimming nearby.'"

"Hmm," Emma said. "And it says that even though it's a remote place, the island has had a lot of commercial activities in the past centuries—coal mining, fishing..."

"Yeah, but no settlements have lasted more than a few years. And now it's uninhabited except for people working with the NPI."

"The NPI?"

"See, up here it says that the NPI stands for Norwegian Polar Institute."

Emma attempted the Norwegian version: "Norsk Polarinstitutt."

"Wait a minute," Sarah said, eyes wide. "Wasn't that the place that Gary Hammock was talking about the last time we ate at the Banana Hammock, remember?"

Emma nodded. "Yeah, it sure is."

CHAPTER 18

Sarah pulled her cell phone from her pocket.

"What are you doing?" Emma asked.

"Calling Adam." Sarah tapped a few buttons and put the phone up to her ear. After four rings, he picked up.

Once Adam was on the line, Sarah said, "Adam, I need to talk to you."

"Sarah, what's going on?"

"You know that partial shoe print?"

"Now, Sarah—"

"Hear me out. That print belongs to Kacey."

"Sarah, Kacey is a friend. How do you know it was her? Could have been someone else with those same shoes."

"They aren't sold in the U.S. They're only available in Norway, and her dad goes there every year."

Adam was silent a moment. "Didn't Gary Hammock come back from his trip to Norway *after* Critsworth's incident?"

It was Sarah's turn to think. "That's true, but..." Sarah shifted on the bed, propping herself up with her free hand. "Gary said he takes the trip almost annually. He could have bought those shoes for her last year. And she lied about not being at the B&B."

"Okay, so she could have been at the B&B, as you suggest. But even if she was there, that doesn't mean she killed Frederick. Where's her motive?"

"That's the thing, I found a bad review of the Banana Hammock Frederick had published a year ago. It was a preview, and he was back in town again, and this time, I think Kacey wanted to stop him before he published another bad review. The Banana Hammock isn't as busy as it's been in past years. Maybe a spike when peak season starts, but even now it's half-full at best during dinner time. Another bad review and they could be sunk."

"Hmm," Adam said, and there was silence on the line again.

"Adam, don't you see? Kacey was at the B&B—"

"She could have been there any time."

Sarah eyed Emma, who was leaning in to hear what Adam was saying on the other end. Then it dawned on her. "Wait," Sarah said. "I remember that we had showers the evening of the murder. I had a hard time getting Winston to go outside to go potty because he hates getting wet. He didn't go until around bedtime. Which means—"

"—the prints were made *after* the showers. Okay, so she was there after the storm and before we took that snapshot of the print. That is quite the coincidence."

"Yeah, and when I asked her when she was at the B&B last, she said it's been ages. Though I caught her give a weird look, then correct herself."

"You are good at reading people."

"It's my job."

Adam let out a huff. "Okay, well, I'll have to take her down to the station for questioning then."

"...if she's still at the restaurant. I hope I didn't spook her."

"You're right, she could run."

Emma raised her eyebrows at Sarah and motioned that she should go. Sarah nodded at her cousin and said into the phone, "I'm right down the street from her. I could go back over and make sure she stays there until—"

"Go," Adam said, cutting in. "I'll be there in ten."

"Okay," Sarah said, and they ended their call, and she glanced up at Emma. "I'll be right back."

Sarah rushed from the bedroom and down the hall past the kitchen. Grandma called after her. "Where are you going? We need to get started on the frosting!"

"Sorry, Grandma, I'll be right back," Sarah yelled over her shoulder as she made it to the door that led to the stairs.

Down the steps she went, and before she knew it, she was out on the main strip. She jogged down the sidewalk toward the Banana Hammock, hoping that Kacey was still there.

What if she'd already fled? She had looked spooked enough to do so...

Heart racing, Sarah blasted off into a sprint, pushing those thoughts aside as she reached the parking lot of the Bar and Grill.

Slowing her pace, she felt her heart pounding in her temple. What if Kacey was already gone? She'd had plenty of time to pack up and run, and she would be far gone, miles away by now. She was getting ahead of herself.

Sarah stepped toward the entrance, and saw that the hostess station was empty. Scanning the restaurant, there was no sign of Kacey.

She spotted Flo in the back of the restaurant. The woman's eyes widened slightly when she saw Sarah.

"Where's Kacey?"

Flo shrugged. "I think she's back here..."

Sarah forged past the hostess station and watched as Flo disappeared into the kitchen. A few moments later, she was relieved when Kacey strode out of the kitchen confidently.

"Sarah," Kacey said. "What are you doing here again?"

Sarah pulled her phone from her pocket. Swiping through her pictures, she came across the picture of the footprint, and held the phone up to show Kacey.

"I found this," Sarah said. "It's a shoe print that was found in the sand outside the B&B shortly after Frederick Critsworth was strangled there. The print has the exact same logo as the sole of your sneaker. I thought you said you weren't there..."

"Oh, c'mon, Sarah. That could be anyone's footprint."

"No way. This particular shoe is not even available in the U.S. It's a rare logo from Bear Island, in Norway—where your dad visits every year. And the shoe is not even made anymore now that the island is no longer inhabited."

Kacey's face turned white as her stance tightened. "That's preposterous. How did you—"

"I saw you wearing the shoe earlier when you were helping Flo, after she spilled her tray. So, tell me, friend to friend, were you at the B&B the night of Critsworth's death?"

Kacey's face flushed, and she took a few steps back as if ready to run out the rear of the restaurant. "I...I...I was there, but—"

Just then, the front door to the restaurant slammed open and two officers approached Kacey in a bustle of movements. A few of the patrons who were eating in the restaurant gawked at the scene that was unfolding.

Kacey's eyes went wide, and she gasped. "What the—"

"Kacey Hammock," one of the officers said, voice booming. "We're taking you in for questioning."

"What?" Kacey's face bore a look of shock. She gawked at the officers, eyes wide, then fixed her gaze on Sarah. Her face now beet red, she grimaced. "It's not what you think."

As she was led out by the men, her eyes were still glued to Sarah.

"I thought you were my friend!"

CHAPTER 19

*S*arah stood near the hostess station and watched as the two officers walked Kacey out the front of the restaurant.

Her friend's words repeated in her mind: *"I thought you were my friend."*

She wasn't proud. She had hoped that it wasn't Kacey, but all signs pointed to her. Emma was right, how well do you really know a person?

Turning around, she noticed the patrons were still gawking, and Flo was stepping into the kitchen, probably wondering how she would handle the rest of the day working the restaurant, down a staff-member. Of course, with the restaurant at less than half capacity, the remaining crew would probably be just fine.

Stepping out of the restaurant, Sarah saw Kacey was being escorted to the police cruiser and put into the back seat.

She strode along the sidewalk, back toward the boutique. It was more than likely Emma had opened the store already. A warm breeze swept through her hair and the world seemed quieter than usual on the boardwalk.

When she got to the boutique, she opened the door to see Emma waiting behind the counter.

"What happened?" Emma asked, shuffling closer.

"They apprehended Kacey in front of everyone."

"That won't be good for business."

"No, I suppose not."

Just then, the door to the apartment opened and Grandma appeared, hands on her hips. "What is going on, Sarah? You were supposed to help me make the icing for the cake."

"They arrested Kacey," Emma said.

Grandma's mouth dropped. "What? Why?"

"For the murder of Frederick Critsworth," Sarah said. "They had enough evidence to take her in."

"Oh, dear." Grandma put a hand up to her mouth. "That's a shame." She shook her head.

"So, now what?" Emma asked Sarah.

"I guess all we can do is wait and see what Adam finds out."

Grandma walked over to Sarah, a concerned look on her face. "Are you all right?"

Sarah dropped her gaze. "Yeah, it's just..." Sarah started and then paused.

Grandma tried to make eye contact with Sarah. "Well, now, what is it?"

Sarah lifted her head. "It's just that Kacey said that she thought I was her friend as the police dragged her out of the restaurant. I guess I just feel bad."

Emma lifted her eyebrows. "Wow, that's rough."

Grandma waved Emma's words away and put her hand on Sarah's shoulder. "You can't blame yourself for that. You didn't do anything wrong. If the evidence all points to her and she did it, well, we can't have a murderer running among us."

"Yeah, Sarah," Emma said, "Grandma's right. Just sounds to me like she was trying to make you feel guilty. Don't let it get to you."

Sarah gave a slight smile and nodded. They were right. She couldn't let it get to her. She didn't murder anyone. She had nothing to be ashamed of. But there was something in the back of her mind nagging her. She wasn't sure what, but maybe it was just the guilt she felt.

Just then, Winston came up to her and nudged her

with his nose and then sat there, looking up at her patiently. They all knew what that meant.

"Did you feed them yet, Sarah?" Grandma asked.

"No, with everything going on, I forgot."

"Well, why don't you feed them, and you can help me finish the cake. Keep your mind busy."

Sarah turned to Emma. "Want me to feed Misty too?"

"Sure. Thanks."

Sarah strode upstairs with Winston and Rugby at her heels. When she got to the kitchen, Winston nudged her again.

"I know, I know..." Sarah said, stepping into the kitchen. She poured kibble into their bowl, then cut up some fresh carrots to place on top. Rugby would eat practically anything, though Winston was a bit pickier when it came to the food selection. The carrots prompted him to start to dig in, and he didn't stop until the bottom of the bowl could be seen.

Sarah got a can of Misty's food and cracked it open, spooning the food out into a dish. She placed the dish down and Misty swept past it. She circled it again, but didn't seem to be interested. Once Winston was done with his food, he moseyed toward Misty's bowl. Sarah figured he was about to eat it, but instead, he sat, as if guarding it.

Sarah gave them a quizzical look. "These animals are

sure acting strange lately…this is the second time he's done this," Sarah said to her grandmother, who was checking the cake.

"Hm?" Grandma said, turning around. "Oh, that?" She chuckled. "Looks like he's guarding Misty's food."

"That's what it looks like to me too. Maybe he's guarding it from Rugby." Sarah put a finger to her chin. "Come to think of it, I am a bit surprised he hasn't eaten Misty's food since we've been here. That dog eats everything."

Grandma and Sarah exchanged a glance and burst into laughter. Then Grandma said, "The cake is almost cooled down. Let's get back to work."

Sarah put her apron back on, and they worked on finishing the cake, piping chocolate cream cheese buttercream icing around the edges and stacking fresh strawberries on top. Grandma took some chocolate she had melting on the stove and drizzled it over the strawberries.

Sarah stepped back, eyeing the cake. "Wow, it's like a masterpiece."

"Wait until you taste it."

Sarah licked her lips. "I don't know if I want to cut it just yet. It's too beautiful."

"I'm surprised Emma wasn't up here hassling us for a taste of the icing."

"I should probably go down there and help her."

Grandma got a knife out. "Not until we take a bite of this cake."

"Hold on," Sarah said, taking out her phone. "Let me take a picture." Sarah stepped forward, holding her phone out with both hands. She snapped a few pictures. "Okay, now we can cut it."

Grandma sliced through the pillowy, soft cake, transferring each slice onto a small plate. Sarah grabbed two forks, one for Grandma and one for herself. They each cut the tip of their cake with the side of their fork.

"All right," Grandma said with a smile. "Now for the taste test."

They took their first bites together and Sarah closed her eyes. The cake was so soft and moist, and there were multiple mini chocolate chip explosions with each bite. The crisp strawberries gave a good balance to the thick, dark chocolate.

Grandma, still chewing, put her finger up. She swallowed and said, "I forgot the milk." She walked over to the fridge while Sarah got two glasses. Grandma poured the ice-cold milk and the glasses fogged with condensation within seconds.

Once Sarah was done with her cake and her milk, she rubbed her stomach. "Well, that did it. I'm definitely feeling better now."

Grandma smiled. "Nothing a good chocolate cake can't fix." She picked up the knife and sliced another piece.

Sarah gave her an incredulous look. "Don't tell me you're going for a second piece! I'm so full."

"No, dear, we don't want to forget about your cousin." Grandma handed the plate with a slice of the triple-layer strawberry chocolate cake to Sarah. "Give this to Emma for me, please."

Sarah took the plate.

"Oh, and let's not forget about the milk again," Grandma said, and poured another glass of milk and gave it to Sarah.

Sarah walked down the stairs to the boutique carefully, as to not spill the milk. When she reached the door, she balanced the plate on her forearm, attached to the hand holding the milk, and opened the door. Sarah scanned the shop but didn't see any customers. Emma was still behind the counter, and she was on the boutique's cordless phone.

"Okay, can you read the order back to me?" Emma said into the phone. She said "uh huh" a few times, then said, "Actually, can we make that two orders of the puppy paw assorted collars?" After a moment, she said, "Thank you," and hung up the phone.

She looked up and a smile spread across her lips. "It's done already?" She took the plate as Sarah put down the milk in front of her. Emma gripped the fork and shoveled a generous piece of cake into her mouth.

"Mmm," she said, still chewing. "This is amazing."

CHAPTER 20

*L*ater that day, Sarah and Emma were down in the boutique, watching after the store while Grandma ran her morning errands. Though the boutique was usually bustling, there seemed to be a trend where customers flooded in and there was a rush. Then there was a period of down time when nobody came in for about an hour, and that tended to occur often in the morning and during lunchtime. Emma seemed to like the down time, so she could get caught up with other work, but for Sarah, it was a bit boring.

Sarah ran a rag along the top of the counter and wrinkled her nose. "Grandma's right," she said. "This place needs to be dusted more often."

Emma was on her favorite stool behind the counter, typing away on her laptop. She stopped typing, glanced at Sarah, and shrugged. Moments later, her fingers continued tapping on the keys.

"What are you working on?" Sarah asked, trying to spark conversation.

"My regular work," Emma said, voice monotone. "Someone's got to reply to all these e-mails we're getting."

"Is the online shop operational now?"

"Yeah. Though I still have a lot of work to do to update the stock levels and such. I'd like to make it automated, so we enter our inventory into an online program that helps keep our site updated. The last thing we want is for someone to buy something on our site when we don't physically have it in stock."

"That makes sense."

"Yeah. It's a work in progress. But I'm also replying to a few companies that might be able to help us manufacture Grandpa's products."

"Oh, that's cool."

"It's a pain in the butt," Emma said, bluntly.

"When are we going to launch that line?"

"Could be months yet. There's a lot to this, Sarah. I'll have to get you in the loop sometime soon. I'm swimming in work."

Looking at her cousin, Sarah could tell Emma was working herself into the ground. She had real dedication to the boutique and helping Grandpa get his new line of pet products to take off.

Winston whimpered nearby.

"What's his problem?" Emma asked.

Spotting Winston sitting outside Grandpa's office door, Sarah said, "I think he wants Grandpa to be here."

"When will he be back from his trip?"

"Any day now."

"Good. I could use his help here," Emma said.

"I know, but Grandpa needs to have his fun. He deserves it."

"Yeah, he does."

Just then, the front door bell jingled and a sharp-dressed man with black hair came in, with a brown toy poodle leading the way.

"Oh, hey, Mr. Fujimoto." Sarah stepped out from behind the counter to greet the owner of the Board Wok sushi bar.

"Hi, Sarah. You can call me Yuki."

Sarah nodded. Yuki's poodle had long, slender legs and an adorable poodle cut. "Of course, Yuki. And this must be Ralph." Upon her saying the dog's name, Ralph wagged his tail and let out a bark. "Mind if I give him a biscuit? We've got Fudderdog treats that I think he might like."

"Sure," Yuki said.

Sarah strode back over to the counter, where Emma continued to work, and reached into the open fishbowl-style container that held the individual treats. As she rummaged through them, Rugby and Winston raced toward the counter, both wagging their tails at the sound. They ignored the poodle, intent on getting a treat.

Sarah gave each of them a treat, then got a third biscuit for Ralph.

"Here you go, boy," Sarah said, handing Ralph the Fudderdog treat. Looking up at Yuki, she said, "These are made by a baker right here in Cascade Cove. I'm not sure if you've met Henry Fudderman yet."

"The man who looks like Santa Claus?"

"That's him."

"Oh yeah, then I have met him. He makes a wonderful fudge cake."

"That's one of my grandpa's favorites."

Yuki smiled, then scanned the displays. "Oh, are these your sweaters?"

"They sure are," she said, walking alongside Yuki until they reached the display of Sarah's creations. "They are hand-knitted."

Yuki reached out to touch one of the sweaters. "Who knitted them?"

"I did."

Yuki's eyes went wide. "You made these?"

"Yes, is there anything you're looking for in particular?"

Yuki picked up one of the sweaters, feeling its soft stitches. "These are beautiful." He turned to Sarah. "Well, Ralph does have a certain style. He always looks dashing in navy blue or deep red."

Sarah smiled. "I can see that, and I might have just the sweater for him. I just finished it and haven't had the time to put it on the shelf yet. I think it's just the right size, too."

Sarah went back behind the counter and picked up the sweater, holding it up for Yuki to see. It was a dark blue argyle sweater with red and gray diamonds going down the back.

Yuki seemed impressed. "That might be just Ralph's style."

"Go ahead and try it on him," Sarah said, handing Yuki the sweater.

Sarah helped Yuki put the sweater on Ralph. He was a fine dog that not only stood still while they put the sweater on, but was helpful by giving his front paws to Sarah and Yuki, so they could put them through the leg holes of the sweater. Once they got it on him, they both took a step back and admired how stylish he looked in it. Ralph lifted his chin, which made his chest puff out a bit, proud and confident.

"Very handsome," Yuki said.

"He seems to really like it," Sarah said.

"I'll take it. And a box of the Fudderdog treats. I haven't seen Ralph enjoy a biscuit like that in a long time."

"You got it. Which flavor?"

Yuki strode over to the display of treats and picked up a box of the peanut butter flavored biscuits. "This'll do."

"Good choice," Sarah said. "By the way, if ever you need a specific sweater made or you see a design you like on the shelf but you can't find it in Ralph's size, let me know. I do custom orders as well."

Yuki smiled. "Thank you very much, Sarah. I may do that. He has a show coming up and I might need something made."

"Great! Just let me know a few weeks ahead of time and bring Ralph in so I can do some measurements." Sarah rang out Yuki and placed the Fudderman treats in a bag. "We'll be back for more sushi rolls soon."

Emma, who was next to her, still on her laptop, nodded and said, "We sure will. Those rolls were incredible."

"Thanks," Yuki said, taking the bag from Sarah. "I'll see you all soon, then. Have a nice day."

"You too."

Sarah watched as Yuki led Ralph out of the store, and the bell jingled as he exited to the main strip.

Emma closed her laptop and smiled. "Done."

"You're finished already?"

"Well, I'm caught up with the emails."

Before Sarah could reply to her cousin, her phone blared from her pocket. She pulled it out and saw Adam was calling her. She answered the call. "What's up, Adam?"

"We've been trying to get Kacey to talk, but she won't say anything."

"What? Why not?"

Emma gave Sarah a confused look.

"She says she'll only talk to you or her lawyer," Adam said.

"Why me?"

"I don't know. She says you understand her more than anyone. To be honest, if you could come down to the station, that would be a better bet than getting a lawyer involved. Maybe you could urge a confession out of her. You two have a long history."

"I've known her since we were young, though I can't

say we were ever best friends or anything. You knew her back then, too."

"I know, but she doesn't want to talk to me. It could be the uniform…"

Sarah considered what Kacey said to her as the police were hauling her out of her own restaurant and took a deep breath. She felt like she owed it to Kacey to at least go down there and talk with her.

"Sarah, can you help us?"

"Okay," Sarah said. Ending the call, she glanced at her cousin. "I hate to do this to you, Em, but I have to go."

CHAPTER 21

own at the police station, Sarah walked into the lobby area. She hadn't been to the station since she was a young girl, when Grandpa Larry got a parking ticket for the Pinto. He tried fighting it, stating that the parking meter must've been broken because he paid for two hours of parking while they visited the downtown museum. He claimed when he got back to the car, they should've had twenty minutes to spare. Said that he timed it with his watch, and was giving her the exact times he left the car and when he came back. The receptionist was kind and gave Sarah a lollipop, but she wasn't letting Grandpa off the hook. Grandpa even went as far as to say that a lollipop for his granddaughter wasn't going to make him go away. It was definitely a memorable day, because Grandpa Larry rarely got angry, but when he did, it used to make her giggle. He always resembled one of those wacky inflatables stationed in front of car lots that waved their arms incessantly for no good reason.

As she scanned the station, she noticed that not much had changed inside. The desk was still facing the entrance and the waiting area was along the wall next to the door.

She walked up to a pudgy man who was now sitting at the front desk. He was eating donut holes from a red cardboard box, and she could see the white powder stuck to the corners of his mouth and his mustache. She wasn't sure if she should say something to him.

Then his eyes shot up, almost startled to see someone standing there. He snatched a napkin and quickly wiped his mouth. "Can I help you, ma'am?"

"Yes, I'm here to see Adam Dunkin."

The man wiped off his fingers and hovered them over his keyboard. "Name?"

"Sarah Shores."

He started typing, then paused and shook his head. "I don't see you in the system. Do you have ID?"

"Uh, well yes, but—"

"I'll need to see your ID, ma'am."

Sarah started digging for her ID when a man came

out from another room. "It's all right, Officer Deats. I'll take Ms. Shores."

Officer Deats shrugged, grabbing another donut hole and popping it in his mouth. He pointed to Adam behind him with his thumb. "Off you go, Ms. Shores." Powder puffed from his lips.

"Thanks for coming down on such short notice," Adam said. They were walking down a long hallway and there were closed doors on either side. "I'm really hoping we can get something out of her."

"Of course."

"But there are a few things I need to go over with you before you go in."

"Like what?" Sarah asked.

"Like, tread lightly in there. Ask as many open-ended questions as you can and keep her talking. Also, try to seem understanding rather than badgering answers out of her. Make her think you are on her side. That you are her friend."

Sarah looked at Adam. "I am her friend."

Adam shook his head. "You know what I mean."

Sarah nodded and was escorted by Adam to a room where Kacey was waiting. She was seated at a rectangular table in a concrete room with a single large mirror set into the wall. Sarah wasn't sure if it was one of those two-way mirrors, but she assumed whatever was said in that room wasn't confidential.

Sarah approached the table where Kacey was seated. She was nervous with the uncertainty of how the conversation was going to go.

Kacey was watching Sarah as she took a seat across the table. Sarah couldn't read her. Her face was expressionless.

"Hi, Kacey," Sarah said.

Kacey stared up at her for a moment, then fixed her gaze on the table that was between them.

"Sarah, I didn't do it."

Sarah didn't know how to respond.

"How could you think that I would have it in me to murder someone in cold blood?"

"Kacey, it's still hard for me to fathom that you could do something like that. But your shoe print and the review from last year—"

Kacey interrupted, "I wanted to tell you the whole story, but I didn't get a chance before they dragged me away."

"Okay," Sarah said, and waited for her friend to continue.

"So, you're right. I lied. I was there that night, but it's not what you think."

"Then, what happened?"

"That review you had cut out of the newspaper? Critsworth wrote that about my father's restaurant last year. We lost a substantial amount of business. Profits dropped almost forty percent. Then Critsworth contacted us after the season was over and said that if we didn't fork over five thousand dollars, he would give us a bad review next year, and our restaurant would sink."

Sarah's eyes went wide.

Kacey continued, "He said that if we gave him the money, in turn he would write an exceptional review, and we would get our profits up and then some. Said we could easily make the money back."

"What did your father say?"

"He refused. He said he built this business from the ground up and no rat was going to try to blackmail him. My father told me personally that we can't let him bully us into giving him money or else he won't stop. But I knew what a bad review from Critsworth could do to a restaurant business."

Kacey took a deep breath, trying to keep her emotions in check, though her flushed cheeks betrayed her.

Kacey continued, "So then Critsworth was back in town, and I decided the only way to save our business was to find the review and steal it the night before he was supposed to submit it. I did some digging to find that out, but it was easy to do a little sleuthing, you know what I mean?"

Sarah nodded, but remained silent.

"He had a tiny laptop at the restaurant, and I saw him fumbling around with a flash drive. I realized that he must be saving his reviews on that device, since he'd been having trouble with his laptop. It would randomly crash, and he'd lose everything, so he kept all his files on that flash drive."

"How did you find that out?" Sarah asked.

"Overheard him talking to one of his 'fans.' Can you believe that monster has fans?"

"Hard to believe. But I'm still confused. Wouldn't he just rewrite it if the flash drive went missing?"

"I thought about that too. At first, I figured his deadline was coming up soon, so he'd be hard-pressed to rewrite it, especially since he would be at the mixer all night. But at any rate, I didn't know what to do. I thought I could delete it, but I didn't want to take any chances of him rewriting it later, so I decided I could alter it to out him as the terrible person he is. But I only got as far as getting the drive from a box in the dresser drawer before I heard someone opening the door to his room at the B&B."

Sarah leaned forward.

"I ran into the closet and hid," Kacey said.

"Who was it?"

"Critsworth, I think. I thought he was at the mixer, but he must've left early. Then a minute later, I heard a knock at his door. Critsworth answered the door and then asked the person what they were doing there."

Sarah's heart pounded. "Do you remember any of what was said?"

"Yeah. Critsworth said, 'Are you following me now? Face it, you're done.' But before he could say anything else, I heard grunting like someone was choking."

Sarah covered her mouth with her hand. She couldn't believe what she was hearing.

"After that, I heard someone fall to the floor. I knew it had to be a body."

"What happened next?"

"Well, when I heard the person leave, I came out and found Critsworth dead. You could imagine my shock." Kacey's eyes welled up with tears, and she began to shake. Sarah reached over and held her hand.

Kacey bowed her head, trying to compose herself.

"Then what happened?" Sarah asked.

Kacey sucked back some tears. "I didn't know what to do. I was afraid if I called the police, they would think I did it. I mean, what was I going to say when they asked me why I was there?"

Sarah took out a tissue from her purse and handed it to Kacey. She dabbed both eyes and thanked her for the tissue.

Kacey continued, "I couldn't just leave the guy there, so I decided to use the old rotary phone by the night-stand, and I snuck out."

"So, you were the anonymous caller?"

Kacey nodded. "I was scared. I didn't know what to do." She put her head in her hands.

Kacey's story made sense, and Sarah needed to get as much information as possible from the person who practically witnessed it.

"Kacey, did you see the person who killed Mr. Critsworth?

Kacey shook her head, tears streaming down her face.

"Did you see anything?" Sarah asked. "Anything at all?"

"No. I froze. Please, help me. You solved the last murder in the Cove."

"Why didn't you call the lawyer?"

"I can't afford one. Only you can help me."

CHAPTER 22

*S*arah rose from her chair, hearing it scrape against the concrete floor. She stepped out of the room, leaving Kacey alone. Adam was standing right outside the door.

"Did you get all that?" she asked Adam after she closed the door behind her.

"Yeah, quite a story."

"You believe her, don't you? I mean, she can't be making all that up."

"It doesn't matter if I believe her or not. I can only go by what the evidence tells me."

She understood where Adam was coming from. She thought a moment. "Do you have a flash drive in your evidence pile?"

"I think we do. We found it on the floor next to the bed by the closet."

"She must have dropped it."

"Yeah, it was probably when she saw the body."

"Well, if she's telling the truth, then there should be an unpublished bad review of the Banana Hammock on that drive."

A chime sound emitted from Sarah's phone. She pulled her cellphone from her pocket and saw she'd received a text message from Emma. All it said was, "Help!" Sarah checked the time and realized it was rush hour at the boutique and no one was there to help her. She hadn't thought she would be that long at the station, and felt bad.

"Listen, Adam," Sarah said, quickly putting the phone back into her pocket. "I've got to go. Can you check the flash drive and let me know if you find anything?"

"Okay. I'll call you as soon as I know something."

Sarah started down the hall toward the front lobby. "Thanks," she said over her shoulder.

Back at the boutique, the bell jingled above Sarah's head as she entered. She scanned the store and saw four different groups of customers and a flustered Emma in the middle, trying to answer a question from one group while ringing out another. Then the phone rang, and Emma's face turned a brighter shade of red.

"I'll get it," Sarah said, rushing to get the phone.

Emma glanced at Sarah, a relieved look on her face. "I saw you come in, but didn't realize it was you," Emma said, words running a mile a minute. "Thought it was another customer—we've been swamped!"

Sarah ignored her cousin and picked up the boutique's phone, a wireless contraption that was a decade or two past its prime.

"Larry's Pawfect Boutique, this is Sarah. How may I help you?"

Sarah helped the person on the phone while simultaneously ringing a customer out. She cocked her head so the phone was secure on her shoulder, and was able to place the purchased items in a bag.

She wrapped up the call and focused all of her attention on the group of customers on the other side of the counter.

"Thanks again," she said to them, and they grabbed their purchases with a smile.

Sarah came out from behind the counter, dodging Rugby and Winston as they mulled about. She approached a woman with her teenaged daughter and greeted them.

Out from behind the pair, a Maltese popped its head out.

"He's adorable," Sarah said.

"She," the teenager corrected.

"What's her name?"

"Mindy."

"Mindy the Maltese—how cute! So, do you have any questions?"

"Mindy needs a new sweater," the woman said.

"Well," Sarah said, reaching a hand out to pull a sweater from the display. She picked out the ivory sweater with the double-cable down the back and cuffs, the one she had just made a couple nights ago. "These are one hundred-percent handmade."

The woman felt the material. "It's so soft. Who made these?"

Sarah smiled. "I did."

"Wow, look at the stitching on this, Carla," the woman said to her daughter, who felt the material and nodded.

"Would you like to try it on Mindy?"

"Sure," the woman said.

Sarah handed the woman the sweater, who crouched and was able to easily put it on her dog.

"Good fit," Sarah said.

The woman checked various parts of the sweater to make sure it wasn't too snug. "It's perfect. I'll take it."

"Anything else today?"

"Just want to browse around. It's our first time in the shop."

"Take your time. And let me know if you have any other questions."

Sarah made her way back to the counter, where Emma was finishing up with the only other group of customers now in the shop.

A few minutes later, Sarah's mother-daughter pair of customers had a few more items they carried to the counter.

"Mindy is getting her own sweater, so I've decided to pick up this shirt for myself," the woman said, placing the article of clothing on the counter.

"Nice selection," Sarah said, looking down at the shirt. She smiled when she saw the cute Maltese dog printed on the shirt, along with the words "Maltese Mama." Though the shirt wasn't handmade like the dog sweaters they had to offer, Sarah remembered seeing this particular design in one of the catalogs from which Emma placed orders for the boutique.

Sarah rang out the rest of their items and let them know their total. She completed the order and bagged the items.

"Thank you!" the woman said, then sauntered out with her daughter and dog flanking her.

Emma stood nearby and let out a huff. "Thanks, you

really swooped in here and saved the day. You certainly know how to multitask."

"What can I say, I'm good like that."

Emma plopped down on her stool and opened her laptop. "You're my hero. Now I can get back to the website work."

Just as the final word came out of Emma's mouth, Sarah's ringtone blared.

Emma eyed Sarah. "Seriously?"

Sarah grabbed her cellphone.

Emma fixed her gaze upward with her hands out, like she was speaking to the ceiling. "I can't wait for Grandpa to come back."

Sarah looked at Emma. "It's Adam."

Emma raised her eyebrows. "Put him on speaker."

Sarah answered the call. "What's up, Adam?"

"Well, Kacey is telling the truth. There is a bad review of the Banana Hammock on the flash drive. Actually, it's damning. You should read what this guy wrote. And I quote, 'The Banana Hammock Burger tastes of what I could only imagine rats would ingest. It was fetid, with an ammonia-like flavor. After only one bite, I felt my entire GI tract prepare to purge.'"

Sarah winced, like someone had struck her in the gut.

Emma tightened her lips. "Gross."

The review was effective. Even she was starting to have second thoughts about ever entering the Banana Hammock again.

"This guy is brutal. He goes straight for the jugular."

"So, are you going to release her?"

Adam exhaled sharply. "Can't."

Sarah shot up from her stool. "What do you mean you can't?"

"Just because she's telling the truth about the bad review he was writing doesn't mean she didn't do it. We have to dig deeper…"

"C'mon, Adam. I think this review speaks for itself. Besides, why would she kill him and take the flash drive? Why not just take the disk?"

"One could argue that she'd kill him because he could simply write another one. She has a clear motive to want him gone, and she was at the scene of the crime around the time of his death."

Sarah shook her head. "But what about what I told you before?"

"What she told you could have been a lie. Think about it—why would she confess to you?"

"You can't hold her forever."

"No, but we can hold her for a little while longer, since she's suspected of a serious crime. We might have something to pin this one down, Sarah. Trust me on this."

Sarah looked at Emma, who shrugged. "He has a point," Emma said.

It was clear to Sarah she wasn't getting anywhere. She'd have to do something, and soon. Otherwise, Kacey might be convicted of a crime she didn't commit.

"Fine," Sarah said. "Hold her, then. But I know I'll find something."

CHAPTER 23

"So, you believe her?" Emma said, her hands on her hips and her head cocked to one side.

Sarah placed her phone on the counter and rubbed her forehead. "Yes, I do. Her story makes sense."

"She could be lying."

"Em, you weren't there. I saw her. She was crying and was visibly shaken, like she went through some kind of trauma."

"Liars can cry. They're called sociopaths."

It was Sarah's turn to put her hands on her hips. "She is far from a sociopath."

"I'm not saying she is one. I'm just saying we should let Adam do his job. I think he knows what he is doing."

"I'm not saying he doesn't. I just think he's wasting

his time chasing a false lead while the real killer is still out there."

"She was there, Sarah. And she has a motive. Adam is doing the right thing keeping her."

Sarah stared her cousin dead in the eyes, as if ready to bore a hole in her. "So, what do you have against Kacey?"

"Nothing. But I call a spade 'a spade,' unlike you."

"What are you talking about?"

"You're blinded by your friendship with her, and there's the fact that you are a very compassionate person. That's why you work so well with kids. It's not a bad thing, but all the evidence points to her. She killed the man—had every reason to, if you ask me—then told you a bald-faced lie. And you fell for it—hook, line, and sinker."

The door to the boutique opened and a handsome, dark-haired deliveryman came in, carrying a large box. He had broad shoulders and biceps that were the size of Sarah's head. "Hey, Emma."

Emma's faced relaxed into a smile. "Hi, Mark."

Mark approached them but his gaze didn't waver from Emma. "I have a package for you."

Oh, boy, Sarah thought. Well, if that wasn't a line from every romcom movie she'd ever seen. She couldn't wait to see how her sassy cousin responded to such a lame line. But Emma remained all smiles and pointed to a corner of the boutique by the front desk.

"You can put it right there," she said. He walked over to the area she was pointing to and bent over, placing the package down lightly.

Sarah scrunched up her face.

When he turned, he pulled a small computer device from where it was hooked to his waist. Still looking at Emma, he handed it to Sarah.

"Oh," Sarah said, taking the device and pulling the stylus pen from the side. She signed for the order and tried handing it back to Mark, but he ignored her.

"So, Emma, did you hear about Veronica's party coming up?" Mark asked.

"Her Epic Annual Spring Break party? Nah, not interested in half-naked girls prancing around in string bikinis and meat-head guys hanging upside down, drinking out of beer kegs."

Sarah placed the mini-computer device down on the counter next to Mark.

Mark rubbed the back of his neck. "Yeah, me neither. That's so lame." He stood there a moment, and there was an awkward silence. "You know, the amusement park is open now."

Emma nodded. "Yeah, they usually open it the first day of this month every year."

"Yeah." He chuckled. "I guess they do." Mark's cell phone buzzed. He checked it quickly and said, "Oh, got to go. The boss is on my tail about getting these deliveries out quicker."

Mark was just about out the door, when Sarah called to him. She had the computer device with the stylus pen in her hand, waving it. Mark checked his waistband, probably out of habit. He jogged over and took the device from Sarah. "Thanks, ma'am," he said, and rushed back out the door.

"Okay," Sarah said to Emma. "What was that?"

"What was what?"

"Mark?"

"Yeah, what about him? He's our delivery guy." Emma shrugged. "He gives me all the latest gossip."

"And what about all the talk about the party and the amusement park?"

Emma planted herself on the stool behind the counter, expression blank. "I don't know."

Sarah smiled. "I think he was trying to ask you out?"

Emma smirked but quickly tried to hide it.

Sarah gasped. "Oh my gosh. You like him."

"We have to get back to work," Emma said, eyeing up the package. It was evident that she was trying to change the subject. "Those are the dog chews—a thousand count, if I remember correctly—but they are all different flavors..."

"So?"

"Well, that means they all have different SKUs. I need to put them in my new system." Emma stayed seated and waited expectantly. "Uh, since you're up..."

"What? You want me to bring the box to you?"

Emma nodded.

"Getting lazier, are we?" Sarah asked.

"Funny, you should quit working here and become a comedian."

"Don't tempt me. You know, I'll be out of your hair after the summer's over. Back in NYC, I'll do my stand-up routine."

"You have a stand-up routine?"

"Did you ever notice how the dots on the ceiling spell out the word 'gullible'?"

Emma craned her neck back, squinting as she stared at the ceiling.

Sarah giggled. She made a show of her trick and bowed. Strolling over to the package, she bent at the knees to hoist it.

"My gosh," she said, feeling its weight in her hands. Her lower back strained, and she dropped the box back down on the floor. She squatted and tried again, this time lifting with her knees.

"You're a weakling," Emma said, shaking her head at Sarah, who was carrying the heavy box over to her.

Sarah plopped it down on the ground next to Emma and let out a huff.

Emma flashed a smile. "It's not like you have to pick it up far from the ground. You're so short."

"I'm not that short. I'm definitely considered average height." Sarah furrowed her brow. "Of course," she muttered.

"Of course, what?"

"I'm a weakling."

"I know that," Emma snickered.

"And Kacey is about the same build as me. Though, she's two inches shorter." Sarah's gaze swept around. "Is Mark still out there?" Sarah ran to the door. She opened it. He was in the doorless truck and was on his cellphone. Sarah whistled loudly, waving Mark back.

He came back in. "Is everything okay with the package?" he asked, looking down at his computer.

"Mark, could you turn around, please?" Sarah asked.

Mark gave a confused look, but then spun around so his back was now facing her.

"When I talked to Adam the first time about this case, he said Frederick was a big guy. Six foot." Sarah regarded Mark, who still had his back to her. "How tall are you, Mark?"

Mark scratched his head. "I don't know. About five-foot-eleven, I guess," he said, throwing a glance back over his shoulder.

"I still don't understand what you're getting at," Emma said to Sarah.

"How tall do you think Kacey is?" Sarah asked.

"I don't know. She's several inches shorter than you."

Sarah put her finger to her chin. "I'd say she's probably between five-one or five-two. Would you agree?"

Emma nodded.

"Okay, Mark, I'm going to try to put my arms around your neck." Sarah reached up, standing on her tiptoes. It took her a moment, but she was able to lock her arms around his neck after a few hops.

Emma shook her head. "It's possible. And besides, she had a rope or something to strangle him with. Height doesn't matter that much then. She can just fling it over his head and pull from behind."

Sarah released her arms and fell back to her feet. "Fine. Hand me a dog leash."

Emma hopped off the stool and sauntered to the wall where they kept the dog and cat leashes.

"May I ask what this is all about?" Mark asked.

Sarah and Emma both hushed him.

Sarah flung the leash over his head, and she missed, smacking him in the back of the head.

"Ow," he said, rubbing his head.

"Well, she'd need to have good aim," Sarah said to Emma, stifling a chuckle.

"Try again," Emma said. She turned to Mark. "Just hold still."

Sarah moved her hands down the leash to give more distance. She steadied herself and swung it over Marks head with success.

"Okay, Mark," Sarah said, "I'm going to pretend to strangle you."

Mark swung around. "What?!"

Emma chuckled. "What? Are you scared?"

He turned to Emma. "I'm not scared."

Sarah tightened her grip, as if she were strangling him. "Just try to shake me off."

"Like this?" Mark bent over and Sarah slid off his back, landing on her butt on the ground.

Sarah got up and was brushing herself off. "A little warning next time?"

"Sorry," he said with a smirk.

"Okay, okay," Emma said. "Fine, so Mark landed you in ten milliseconds. But look at the guy! He's built like an ox."

Mark blushed. "Well, I do work out from time to time."

Sarah ignored him. "Yeah, but Kacey is a couple

inches shorter and Critsworth is a couple inches taller and, not to mention, Critsworth is a big guy. I mean, the guy eats for a living. He could have easily flipped Kacey off his back or banged her into a wall. Even a man like Adam would struggle to pull that off."

"Let's be real. Adam isn't the tallest guy, either," Emma said.

"She'd have to have the upper body strength, too," Mark said. Sarah and Emma both glanced at him. He shrugged. "Hate to say it, but if that is the best you can do, then I doubt she'd be able to do much harm."

Sarah narrowed her eyes at him. "I could have pulled harder."

Mark smiled gently. "I don't mean to offend, Sarah. It's just that you would have had to pull harder than that to close my windpipe."

Mark was right. Kacey just wouldn't have the upper body strength.

"Unless…" Emma tapped her finger to her chin. "She had an accomplice."

Mark nodded and Sarah shot him a look. "You don't even know what we are talking about."

Mark put his hands up. "You're the one who called me in here to be a prop for your demonstration."

"Yeah, and that's all you are—a prop. Now get out of here."

Emma snickered.

Mark gripped his hand-sized computer device and headed toward the door. He glanced over his shoulder at Emma. "Maybe I'll see you at the amusement park sometime?"

"Maybe," Emma said. "But if not, I'll see you here at two p.m.?"

"Always," he said, walking toward the door. When he passed Sarah, he tipped his imaginary hat. "I bid you farewell."

Sarah waved him toward the door.

When he left, Sarah shook her head. He was a real piece of work.

CHAPTER 24

There was an evening rush and Sarah and Emma were busy the rest of the day with customers. Emma seemed to have an extra spring to her step and Sarah chalked it up to the delivery guy, Mark. When everything calmed down again, Misty jumped down from her shelf and rubbed her body against Emma's leg. She bent down and picked her up, petting her long, soft fur. She turned to Sarah.

"Are you going to call Adam tonight after we close?" Emma asked.

Sarah could hear Misty's purring from where she stood. "Yeah, I was waiting all day to call him. I really hope I can talk him into releasing Kacey."

A whining at the office door.

"Winston, no whining."

"What's the matter with him?" Emma asked.

"I don't know. He was doing that the other day. I think he just misses Grandpa."

Emma rose from her stool. "Then I'll just open the door, and he'll see he's not there."

Emma opened the door and Winston took off into the room. In the next moment, the corgi slammed into something.

Sarah hurried into the room and saw that a whole mess of newspapers were scattered about on the floor. She zeroed in on the bookshelf and figured they must've been stacked there from when Grandma was doing her scrapbooking the other day. She always kept them in Grandpa's office because he liked to save old, unused newspapers in case he ever needed them for cleaning windows or packing things in boxes.

"Winston!"

Sarah huffed, and Emma joined her as she got down on her knees to gather the papers. She started to put them back in order the best she could.

"You think Rugby is rubbing off on Winston?"

"I don't know, but this behavior is something I'd expect from Rugby, not Winston." She gave Winston a look, but he sat innocently, panting softly.

Rugby pranced in and sniffed at the papers that had fallen.

Sarah smiled at Rugby. "You heard us talking about you, boy?"

The yellow lab continued his sniffing as they continued picking up the papers and putting them back in order.

"My goodness," Sarah said. "Grandpa is really a pack rat. Some of these papers are from a decade or so ago."

"I know. He acts like newspapers will become obsolete one day, and so he hoards them."

"Won't they?"

Winston let out a small growl and snatched one of the papers. He shook his head, violently.

"No, Winston, don't do that," Sarah said.

Winston gawked up at her, and walked over with the papers in his mouth.

"Drop it," Sarah said, voice stern.

As commanded, Winston released the papers into Sarah's hand.

"Good boy." She patted him on the head.

"Teach him to fetch my slippers in the morning," Emma said, but Sarah ignored her.

Sarah stared down at the paper and flipped it around to find the date, so she could put it in order. "What's this?" she muttered.

"What?"

Sarah's mouth dropped as she read to herself.

Emma, who was on the floor from picking up papers, scrambled on her knees to get closer to Sarah. "Sarah," she said louder. "What is it?"

"It's an article about Frederick Critsworth." Sarah studied the paper. "Listen to this: 'Cruel Critsworth Strikes again in Cascade Cove, sinking another family-owned business with Callous Review.'"

Sarah and Emma exchanged glances, and Sarah continued, "'As Critsworth tries a variety of cuisines, owners tremble in the corner. His column has brought food back to the forefront, spotlighting delicacies in the hot vacation spots, including Cascade Cove. But if your food is not up to par, be prepared to walk the plank. Just ask the Pirate's Deck, a restaurant modeled after a pirate ship. Unfortunately, their business 'sank' after a bad review from Critsworth.'"

"That's terrible."

"Yeah. It goes on. Apparently, Critsworth wrote that their food wasn't good enough for a hungry dog and not worthy of even the least picky of eaters. The article goes on: 'Within weeks, The Pirate's Deck boarded up their doors. From high end cuisines to dives, he reviews them all.'"

"I remember the Pirate's Deck," Emma said. "Honestly, I loved their food, and the people running it were very nice. I don't remember anything about this review."

"I've never seen you read a newspaper."

"No, why would I? Grandpa reads it from time to time, but he mostly throws it in this heap for Grandma."

"Well, there's more…'Most recently, the Crab Shack at Cascade Cove found themselves on the bad side of Critsworth. After a jarring review, where Critsworth described the food as not being fresh, The Crab Shack is struggling to keep their doors open…'"

Sarah glanced at Emma, eyes wide.

"That's Toby's place," Emma said.

"That explains why it seemed so empty when I went over there for coconut shrimp the other day."

"When was this article written?"

"Last year, I think." Sarah looked for the date. Instead, she saw three large words, "For the Kill," with a quote behind it. "Hold on, they have a quote directly from that review here. 'The Crab Shack: Rubber dipped in Butter. Despite what the owner claims, the crabs are not fresh. The meat was rubbery and tasteless. If I wasn't told I was eating crab, I would think I was chewing on a balloon, indefinitely. To put it mildly, gnawing on wadded paper would be more rewarding than the crab meat sold in this establishment.'"

"Wow. He's harsh."

"I'll say." Sarah stood up and put the last of the newspapers on the pile, keeping the ones with Critsworth articles aside.

"What are you going to do?" Emma asked.

"I don't know. But maybe it wouldn't hurt to pay Toby another visit."

CHAPTER 25

Sarah strode along the boardwalk alone until she reached Toby's Crab Shack. Inside, she noticed the place was vacant of customers, as usual.

"Hi, Sarah," Toby said from the back of the restaurant.

His hostess stood nearby, waving, but she exuded boredom. Sarah caught the woman glance at her watch, probably anxious to go home.

Off to the other side of the restaurant, a waitress was on her cell phone, for lack of anything better to do.

"Are you back for more coconut shrimp?" Toby asked. "I'll put you at the best seat in the house."

"Uh, sure," Sarah said, hesitantly. She followed Toby over to a table. He pulled out a chair and she sat down. "Say, Toby…I have a question."

"Ask away."

"I was going through my grandpa's old newspapers and saw a review of your place by Frederick—"

"Oh yeah?" Toby asked, cutting her off. His smile suddenly disappeared.

Sarah swallowed hard, and the man apparently saw that he had frightened her. His facial features loosened up, but she could still tell he was agitated.

"Yeah, the review said that your food isn't fresh."

The veins in Toby's neck bulged. "Not fresh? You've had my food. You know it's fresh. The shrimp and crab are fresh, and so is the fish. In fact, I just caught them this morning. Come and I'll show you," Toby said, waving for Sarah to follow him.

Sarah rose from her chair, feeling a bit uneasy, but she remembered that there were two other people in the dining area. She followed him back into the kitchen.

He opened the large swinging door.

It was an enormous kitchen with lots of counter space, including a middle island for prepping fish. A few ovens lined the one wall, and she could see that one of the ovens was being used for storage. But it was the walk-in freezer that sent shivers down her spine. By the looks of it, he could keep an entire whale in there if he wanted.

At the far end of the kitchen, she could see Toby's

office. It wasn't closed off like she had expected. He led her to the office area, past all the knives and other tools that she wasn't quite familiar with. Some of them bore resemblance to torture devices and were all lined up, hanging on the wall.

"See all these trophies on the shelf? These are some of my best catches," Toby said, gesturing to the shelves that lined the walls of the entire kitchen. They were filled to the brim with fishing trophies. "And here's some pictures—you can see how nice all of these are. And I serve them the same day I catch them, so you know they're fresh. Look, back there, you can see all my fishing gear."

Sarah spotted the gear and asked, "Why is everything out of the tackle box?"

"Had a little accident this morning and my tackle box fell into the water. I'm lucky I got it back at all. I was reeling in a big fish and it dropped in. Just drying out all the contents now."

Sarah inched over to the gear, eyeing it. She picked up a spool of fishing line and her brows furrowed.

Toby said, "That's the best of the best. Many people don't realize how important fishing line is. Everything down to strength, size, color, and so on…"

"I never knew that."

"So, you believe me now?"

"Of course, I believe you, Toby." Sarah gave him a smile. She still felt nervous standing in a room filled with blades and tools that could be used easily as murder weapons. Not to mention, the enormous storage unit, looming right behind her. It was probably best to agree with Toby even if she didn't.

Sarah rubbed her stomach. "Say, I could really use some coconut shrimp right about now."

"C'mon, why don't you go have a seat, and I'll get you the catch of the day?" Toby wore his "salesman" smile and waited for Sarah's response.

"All right," Sarah said. Coconut shrimp or fish. Didn't matter, as long as they got out of the torture room.

Toby led her back out into the dining area. "Super fresh catch of the day, coming right up."

She took a seat and the waitress came over. "Hi," Sarah said to her, but before she could answer, Toby called out to her.

"I've got her food order already, just get her drink order."

Sarah ordered an iced tea, and the waitress strode off to get it for her. A minute later, she was back with the beverage. Sarah took a sip through the straw, the cold tea quenching her thirst.

She scanned the restaurant, but it was still empty except for the two staff members Toby had scheduled for the night. They still appeared bored, but neither came over to strike up a conversation with Sarah.

Seated alone, she pulled out her phone and saw that she'd received a text from Emma.

"I found something you're going to want to see," the message read.

Sarah typed in a reply: "What is it?"

"I'll show you when you come back. Hurry up!"

Sarah tapped her foot. She regretted ordering food, but she didn't want to be rude by leaving abruptly before her food came.

"I ordered food at Toby's place," Sarah texted.

"Don't eat it," came Emma's reply.

Just then, Toby came out with a platter of food and a smile fixed on his face.

"Enjoy!"

"Um, Toby...an emergency came up. Could I get this to go?"

"Just try a bite," Toby said.

Sarah's eyes darted around the restaurant. The waitress and the hostess were nowhere to be found. "Uh, I really should go, Toby. Could you please just wrap it up?"

Toby's smile faded. "Just one bite. I want you to see how fresh the fish is. You'll see that Frederick Critsworth was a liar and a fraud."

Sarah picked up the fork. Emma's text was floating in her head: "Don't eat it." But why not? Sarah was confused, but she knew she should heed Emma's warning.

She cut the fish with the side of her fork and steam came billowing out from it. She had to admit, it looked and smelled delicious.

Toby waited. "Go on. I bet you it's the best fish you ever had."

Sarah swallowed hard as she lifted the fork to her mouth. She glanced up at Toby, who was still waiting, and gave him nervous smile.

He smiled back, anxiously waiting for her to take a bite.

She opened her mouth to take a bite and then said, "You know, could I have some pepper? I simply love pepper with my fish."

"I've already added pepper and lemon. It's to die for, I swear."

Sarah's eyes grew wide. What did he mean by that?

"Go on," he said, "it gives me great pleasure to see the face of my customer after they have their first bite."

"I'm sure it does."

Sarah lifted the fork with the small piece of fish on it to her lips.

He wouldn't poison her. Everyone would know it

was him, right? But was she really willing to take that chance? No, even if he was the murderer, he strangled Critsworth. He didn't poison him.

She opened her mouth again.

Seconds later, her cell phone blared.

"I have to take this," Sarah said, and pulled her phone from her pocket and pressed it to her ear. "Hello?"

She heard Emma's voice. "Hurry up, Sarah."

Sarah rose from her chair, reached into her purse, and pulled out a fifty-dollar bill. "So sorry, but I have to go," she said to Toby, who picked up the cash and huffed in frustration.

"You're missing out, Sarah."

She disregarded Toby as she hurried out of the restaurant and headed back to the boutique.

"This better be good," Sarah said to Emma.

"Don't worry," Emma said. "You'll be as shocked as I am."

CHAPTER 26

*B*ack at the apartment, Sarah rushed up the stairs. When she hurried through the door, Rugby jumped up with the Frisbee in his mouth.

"Not now, Rugby."

Ever since she'd taken him to the beach with the Frisbee, he'd been eager to go again. Too bad he'd been more than a handful that time, and she was not looking forward to another outing with him on the beach. He gave her the puppy-eye look that made her heart sink. "I'm sorry, maybe later."

Grandma called from the kitchen, "Sarah, is that you?"

"Yeah, Grandma."

Grandma came out with her apron on and a tray of brownies stacked like a pyramid. "You want a brownie?"

"Not right now."

"They have those chocolate chips you love." Grandma inhaled the brownies' chocolatey aroma. "And they're fresh from the oven."

"I'll have one later. Where's Emma?"

"I'll tell you if you have a bite of my brownies." Grandma raised the tray.

Sarah stopped and gave her a terrified look.

"What?" Grandma said, a mixture of confusion and concern on her face.

Sarah stomped past her. "What is it with everyone trying to get me to take a bite of their food?" Sarah said, walking down the hall to her room.

"I didn't mean to upset you, dear," Grandma called from the other end of the hall.

Sarah raced into her room to find Emma settled on her bed, legs crossed, with her laptop on her thighs. Sarah closed the door and Emma peered back at her.

"What's going on out there?" Emma said.

"Why shouldn't I eat Toby's food?"

"Um, why would you?" Emma asked, furrowing her brow. "He could be a murderer."

"That's it?" Sarah said. She was about to lose her mind. "You mean, you didn't find something on Toby that would make you suspect he would poison me with fish?"

"No, just imagined you'd have the common sense to not eat it, just in case."

"Seriously, Em? You are unbelievable. I probably made a complete fool out of myself." Sarah perched herself on the edge of the bed, putting both hands through her hair. "I didn't ask all the questions I wanted to because you had me scared half out of my wits."

"Sorry, I guess. But you should see what I found."

That's right. Sarah almost forgot that Emma said she had found something. It might not have been anything dealing with Toby poisoning food, but she was curious to find out what it was.

Emma scooted up closer to Sarah with her computer. "So, I was going through all the reviews Critsworth has published in the past fifteen years."

"And..."

"Well, let me tell you. This guy has made quite a name for himself. He only gives restaurants a rating of A or F."

Sarah furrowed her brow. She wasn't sure what Emma was getting at.

Emma continued, "It's part of his shtick. His extreme reviews are what make him popular."

"Makes sense. These days you have to be extreme to be noticed and gain popularity."

"Right," Emma said. "That is, unless he does one of

those 'preview' reviews of a restaurant he will revisit for a full review later."

"What do they get?"

"An average review. Sometimes it's leaning more toward bad, but usually, it's pretty average. But we'll revisit that in a moment, because this guy has more power than you think."

Sarah couldn't understand how a food critic would have a lot of power. Sure, he could give a bad review and the restaurant could be slow for a while. But she was sure, with even the awful reviews she'd read by him, most restaurants could bounce back. After all, it was only one man's opinion.

"I found this." Emma adjusted her laptop so Sarah could see the screen. There was a list of restaurants that Critsworth had reviewed, and they had a tiny red "x" next to them or a green check mark.

"What's this?"

"Remember how he gave the Pirate's Deck a bad review, and they closed their doors the following year?"

"Yeah, but that was one restaurant. It could have had nothing to do with Critsworth's review, or maybe they closed their doors for other reasons. We don't know." Then Sarah remembered what Kacey had said to her. How she knew what a Critsworth review could do to a restaurant business. Surely, Sarah didn't think she meant close their doors. But Kacey had apparently been eager to get her hands on that review, so much so that she'd broken into someone's room, rummaged through their stuff, and stolen it.

"Really, Sarah? Did you read those reviews? What about the review he was writing about the Banana Hammock?"

"Of course. It was terrible."

"Now, imagine you're a tourist about to visit the beach and you don't know the area. You want to know what restaurants are good. If you look it up on your computer, the first review that comes up is Critsworth. Are you going to give a restaurant a chance after some popular critic writes that the food made him want to hurl?"

"Point taken."

"This man determines whether a restaurant fails or succeeds." Emma pointed to the screen. "Just about every single 'F' he gives, a restaurant closes within one year. And every restaurant that got an 'A' is not just succeeding—they're thriving."

Sarah's mouth dropped as Emma scrolled down the page, revealing all the restaurants that had failed after a bad Critsworth review.

Then an idea hit Sarah like a sack of bricks. "Wait, so the average previews..."

"Yeah, if Kacey is telling the truth, then he might be doing these quick sneak peek reviews to give those restaurants a taste of what he can do."

"And he blackmails them."

"For thousands of dollars," Emma said. "And there's more."

Sarah furrowed her eyebrows. "There is?"

"Yup." Emma clicked on another tab. On it was a website that appeared to be at least twenty years out of date.

"What is this?"

"It's a website that archived old websites back in the day. By using this, you can kind of look back in time."

"Okay…"

"I just wanted to see how far back these reviews went, so I went on here and I found something interesting. Here, check this out."

Emma clicked on another link and pulled up an old review from an ancient-looking website. She pointed to the bottom of the review, next to Critsworth's name.

Sarah's mouth dropped. "Are you telling me…"

Emma eyes lit up. "He had a partner."

CHAPTER 27

"So, Kate Thompson was Critsworth's partner?" Sarah asked, still staring at the screen. "Who is she?"

"I don't know," Emma said, "but I did a wide search looking for anything about her background."

"And?"

"Couldn't find much."

"Can't you find it on this website time-machine thingy?"

"They only recover so much. Besides, looks like this was from before the time Critsworth became well known as a food critic."

"So…it could mean nothing?"

"I don't know. Just found it odd that he had a partner

who seemed to fall off the face of the earth. I thought maybe you should know. Maybe it relates to the investigation. After that, though, I hit a dead end. I couldn't find anything else."

Sarah crossed her arms. "No crazy story or hypothesis this time?"

"Got nothing."

A wrinkle creased Sarah's brow. She couldn't go back to Toby's Crab Shack and do more digging. She recalled her conversation with him, retracing her steps in the Crab Shack. The kitchen. The knives. Then she thought about all the fishing gear that was laying out to dry from his tackle box. "I think I know what he used to carry out the deed."

"You think it was Toby?" Emma asked.

"I would bet on it."

"But we didn't even find out if he had an alibi that night."

Emma was right. That was one bit of information she was supposed to get out of him tonight, and didn't. She didn't want to make a fool of herself again like she had with Mrs. Montgomery. It would be too embarrassing, but she'd have to take the risk.

"I'm betting on the fact that his restaurant closes by 9 p.m. and he has no immediate family to go home to," Sarah said.

Emma furrowed her brows. "Now, that's not very concrete, even by our standards. He could have been anywhere. You know, it's always the last person you suspect or someone you never suspected at all."

"Like who?"

"I don't know," Emma said, tapping her chin. "His old partner?"

Sarah put her hands on her hips, waiting. She wasn't buying it. "So, you think it was Kate Thompson now?"

"Don't you think it's kind of suspicious that we can't find anything on this lady? It's like she only exists as a byline on his old reviews, before he was famous. Then, suddenly, she's nowhere to be found. Maybe he did something to her that—"

"Are you hearing yourself right now? You don't even know what she looks like—maybe she's a private person and the fact you can't find anything about her has a perfectly good explanation. I'd say you *are* jumping to conclusions..."

The door swung open. "You two girls fighting again?" Grandma was standing at the door. She wasn't wearing her apron anymore, and Sarah assumed she must have been in her room, which was next to Sarah and Emma's. "What is going on?"

"It's nothing," Emma said. "Just that Sarah doesn't think that a woman who used to be Critsworth's partner, and then disappeared without a trace fifteen years ago, has anything to do with his murder."

Sarah shook her head. "Emma, we got our guy. He's a fisherman, which means he's strong, and he has motive—"

"Girls," Grandma said, hands on her hips. "Emma, who is this woman you're talking about?"

"Her name is Kate Thompson."

Grandma tapped her chin. "I don't know a Kate Thompson, but the name does sound awfully familiar."

"She used to be partners with Frederick Critsworth, writing reviews."

"Is she local?"

Emma sat up straight and clicked on her keys. "That's an idea! Maybe I can find her in the local archives, somehow." Emma typed feverishly. "It's a long shot, but if they did a review together in Cascade Cove, they might have a picture of her."

"Grandma, don't encourage her," Sarah said. "This woman could be living somewhere else—doing something else. Living a new life."

"There's no harm," Grandma said. "I'm just curious. Usually, I can place a name with a face, and this one—"

"I think I found something," Emma said.

Grandma and Sarah stopped and glanced at each other.

"Uh, I think you all need to see this," Emma continued, turning her laptop, so they could see.

"What?"

"I think I found who Kate Thompson *really* is. Last name is Gerkins—and you'll never believe what her first name is…"

Sarah and Grandma both studied the screen. There was a picture of a smiling woman they all knew well.

Sarah's mouth dropped. "No way…"

"Well, I'll be," Grandma said. "It's no wonder I couldn't put the name to a face."

Emma turned to Grandma. "Yup. Looks like our little friend here had a pen name back then."

"Now it all makes sense," Sarah said.

"Now do you think she had something to do with Critsworth's murder?"

"I'm not sure, but I have an idea that might give us that answer." Sarah got up from the bed. "But I'm going to need your help." She pointed to Emma. "Can you call Toby?"

"Sure, no problem."

"I'll tell you exactly what to say," Sarah said. She turned to Grandma. "And I'll need you to call Adam."

"I can do that," Grandma said.

Sarah walked toward her suitcase and dug through the piles of clothing that were lying around it in heaps on the floor until she found a dark hoodie. She gave it a whiff and crinkled her nose slightly. It would do. She held it up.

"I have a plan."

CHAPTER 28

Sarah felt the warm air cascade into the hood that concealed most of her face. Next to her stood Emma, who she could see beneath the overhead light at the end of the boardwalk. It was now close to 11:00 p.m. and the area was desolate.

"I don't know about this, Sarah," Emma whispered, her voice barely audible above the crashing high-tide waves.

Sarah hushed her. "Be quiet. And stop fidgeting. We have to appear to be confident."

"How can I be confident when I don't know if this is going to work? A lot could go wrong."

"Trust me," Sarah said. Though, she wasn't sure she trusted herself at the moment. Emma was right. A lot could go wrong.

They waited a bit longer before Sarah started to get antsy herself. "You called him and told him to meet us here?"

"Yeah. Told him eleven o'clock, like you said." Emma pulled out her phone and checked the time. "He should be here at any moment," she said, slipping the phone back into her pocket.

Suddenly, a figure lurched out from the shadows, and Sarah recognized the man. His smile still resembled that of a used-car salesman, though when he saw her face, a look of shock appeared.

"Sarah," Toby said. "What in the world are you doing out here?"

"I could ask you the same thing..."

"Well, I was out for a walk."

Sarah took a step closer. "I don't think so. I think it's quite the coincidence that you'd receive an 'anonymous' call from someone who knew what you did to Frederick Critsworth, and then you show up at the exact place at the precise time that the mysterious person tells you to."

Toby's face turned red. "It was *you*?"

Sarah nodded.

"Why would you think it was me?" Toby asked.

"I didn't at first, but then I thought about that story you told me about how your father gave you the restaurant after he died. You loved your father so much that you wanted to keep his legacy."

"That's because I work hard, just like he did, getting up in the wee hours of the morning and every weekend to catch fresh fish for my restaurant."

"Yes, but you didn't take your boat out the weekend of the murder. Took me a while to remember that you didn't have an alibi for the entire weekend. The same weekend Critsworth was murdered. I overheard you talking to Erwin in the boutique a few days ago."

"I was sick."

"That's right. You said you came down with a bug."

Toby clenched his jaw. "You have no proof. No murder weapon."

"But I do. It wasn't until I saw that extra-strong fishing line in your restaurant's kitchen, I remembered a key fact about the marks on Critsworth's neck, and I was able to put it all together. There were no rope burns or anything like that, but marks showing something thinner was used. Like a wire...fishing wire, to be exact. Your fishing line was the best of the best, Toby...at more than just catching fish. It did the trick for murder."

"That's ludicrous," Toby said.

"Is it, though? You had the strength, not only being a fisherman but a whaler, like your dad. And, not to mention, you had the motive: the terrible review that nearly sunk your business. So, before Critsworth could submit this year's reviews, you took matters into your own hands."

"You have no evidence whatsoever to prove any of that."

"We have an eyewitness, someone who was hiding in the closet of the Sea Breeze Room at the B&B. They heard you strangling Critsworth and even caught sight of your face." Sarah pulled out her cell phone. "I have them on speed dial, and all I have to do is call them— they'll go down to the station and tell them everything they know…" Of course, Kacey was already down at the station, but Sarah hoped the bluff would cause Toby to utter some incriminating words.

"What do you want? The man was a rat. A repulsive, fat rat who was trying to take me for everything I was worth. I didn't have ten thousand dollars to even give him! And he wrote that disgusting review about my restaurant anyway. He smeared my father and my name by saying the food wasn't fresh. And it put me under. My mother, my poor, sweet mother had to lend me thousands to even keep the restaurant running. She cried every night. He got what he deserved. So, you want to bribe me like Critsworth did? You're crazy if you think I'll play your games!"

Sarah was about to reply when she saw a knife blade

glinting in the light. Sarah put up her hands and Emma followed suit.

"Woah," Emma said, hands trembling.

Now this was becoming serious. Sarah's mind was racing. She needed to mitigate the situation before things got out of hand and one of them got hurt. Or worse, killed. "Toby, don't do this. What would your father think?"

"He wouldn't think anything. He's dead." Toby advanced toward them, and Sarah and Emma took a step back. Emma shot a glance at Sarah, her eyes asking, *What do we do now?*

"What about your mother?" Sarah asked him.

"She won't know anything about it. No one will. I'll take care of you both and no one will ever figure it out. Just like the police, who couldn't figure out what happened to Critsworth. They weren't even close until you came and stuck your nose where it didn't belong." Sarah's mind was racing. Did Grandma call Adam like she was supposed to? She knew her grandma would have—she wouldn't let them down. She made sure Grandma waited until after they left so that it would buy them time to talk to Toby, because she knew that Adam wouldn't let her talk to him alone. But she also knew he wouldn't talk if the police were there. Now, she thought they couldn't get there fast enough.

Toby took another step toward them. "Sarah, we could have been friends. It didn't have to go down like this."

"Toby, put the knife down," came a woman's voice. It sounded like it was coming from the shadows just beyond a wooden bench.

Toby's gaze swept to see who it was. For a split-second, Sarah thought about trying to knock the knife out of his hand, but she stood frozen. What if she missed? Footsteps approached and a figure emerged from the shadows. When the light illuminated the person, Sarah's mouth dropped.

It was the woman from the picture they had found on Emma's computer.

"Flo?"

lo Gerkins, from the Banana Hammock, was standing there. The bouncy, energetic girl who always served them when Kacey wasn't there. Now, she was trying to get Toby to put the knife down.

"Toby, I won't say it again." Flo crept closer to him. "Nobody else needs to get hurt."

"I told you I would take care of this," Toby said to Flo. "Just like I took care of Critsworth for us."

"No, you said you would just handle it. I didn't agree for you to murder two more people."

Sarah remembered when she'd been clipping out the newspaper article about a person named Gerkins when she was helping her grandma with her scrapbooking. And with the picture she saw on Emma's computer, it was now confirmed. "Flo? Flo Gerkins?" Sarah said. "So, you really are Kate Thompson?"

Flo turned to Sarah. "That was a lifetime ago. It was a pen name when I wrote reviews with Critsworth. I didn't think it would be you two coming out to meet Toby," Flo said. "I thought it was someone else trying to blackmail him. He called me right after he got off the phone with you."

"Be quiet, Flo," Toby said.

Before another word could be uttered, Sarah saw movement to her left. Two officers flanked Adam, and they all had guns drawn.

"Drop your weapon!" Adam shouted.

Toby glanced at the officers, and gripped his fishing knife tighter.

"Drop it, now!"

Toby hesitated for another moment—one that felt like an eternity to Sarah—then complied. He bent over and placed his weapon on the ground and eased back from it.

"You've got nothing on me," Toby said.

"We heard everything. A lot of incriminating things," Adam said. "Plus, we have two witnesses right here." He nodded toward Sarah and Emma, who still had their hands up. "You can put your hands down now."

Sarah's gaze zeroed in on Flo, who had put her hands

on her face and started to sob. "I didn't mean for this to happen," Flo said.

"I know," Sarah said, "but you've been nervous about getting caught ever since his death. You even dropped all those drinks at the Banana Hammock when I was there last. You were leaning in to hear what I was saying about the murder case and leaned a little too far."

"He was an awful man," Flo said.

Sarah pulled the printed article from her pocket. "Oh, you don't have to tell me. I know what Frederick did to you—I have all the details right here in an old article we printed off the internet. Just as Critsworth was starting his rise to fame, he gave you the boot. While he went on to be a household name, and gain all the wealth he had, you were thrown to the curb."

"No, you don't understand. That's not the whole story. I could have been someone."

"What happened?"

"Critsworth and I did the reviews, but we were just ordinary food critics trying to make it. I changed my name to Kate Thompson because it was a better name than Flo Gerkins. We weren't well known, and we weren't making much money at all. In fact, we both had other jobs to make up the difference. But then Frederick came up with the idea to be more polar with our reviews in order to stand out. I thought it was a great idea, and we started gaining popularity until he started doing these 'sneak peek' reviews that were average. I didn't understand why he was doing that. When I confronted him, he told me that we could make a lot of money by doing average reviews for a restaurant, and then give them the option of giving them a good review or a bad review in exchange for money."

"Blackmail," Sarah said.

Flo nodded. "I told him that's what it was and I would have no part of it, and that I was going to report him if he kept doing it."

"What did he do?"

"He laughed and said, 'Too bad.' The next day, there was an article in the paper about me and how he wasn't partners with me anymore because of shady and distasteful business propositions that I was proposing and arranging. He stated that he caught me blackmailing restaurants in exchange for a good review! He completely smeared my name, and my dreams of being a food critic were drained into a garbage disposal and ground up. No one would ever trust me."

"So you had to get even. And you used Toby to pull it off, since he had a reason for Frederick Critsworth to be out of the picture as well."

"Frederick deserved it! He stole everything from me," she said, face red and tears streaming down her cheeks.

"Everything he had, he stole by destroying my career. He went around spreading lies about me, so much that I had to go back to using my real name in order to get a job."

"But I don't understand," Sarah started. "How did you and Toby get together?"

"I knew Frederick Critsworth was coming back after his 'sneak peek' review of the Banana Hammock. Kacey's dad wasn't going to pay him, and I knew he was after me. He wanted to leave me jobless again. I knew what he was going to do to the Banana Hammock. It was my fault and there was nothing I could do to help the people who had become my family. But when I found Toby at Teek's Tiki Bar, down and out about Critsworth's return after what he did to his restaurant..."

Sarah completed her sentence. "You knew Toby had the motive and the strength to do what you couldn't."

"I didn't think he would actually do it. I only proposed the idea. But when he did it, the world felt like a better place. He couldn't hurt anyone anymore, and I could finally live in peace." Flo paused. "I'm sorry, but I don't regret what I did. The man is better off dead."

Flo continued to sob as the officers pulled her hands behind her back and cuffed her. They'd already done the same to Toby, and they escorted the pair away.

Emma wrapped her arms around Sarah. "Are you okay?"

Sarah hugged her cousin back. "I'm fine. You?"

"Peachy."

Adam approached them. "Quite a story."

Sarah was relieved. "Yes. I'd feel sorry for her, but she had other options. Maybe she couldn't have been a food critic again, but she could have told the police that this man was blackmailing Gary, and that he had black-mailed Toby, too."

"She could have," Adam said, "but we would have had to do a lot of investigating, and if there wasn't any paper trail..." Adam shrugged, "...then there wouldn't have been much evidence. Neither man paid him, so we'd have had no proof. Can't arrest him for a bad review."

"Too bad for that," Sarah said. "Some of those reviews were so bad, they were criminal. Anyway, I'm just glad this whole thing is over."

"Me too," Adam said. "Now I can get back to nabbing petty criminals again."

Sarah cracked a smile. "If only the criminals would stick to stealing stuffed animals. What a world that would be."

CHAPTER 30

It was another exquisite day in Cascade Cove and Sarah was relieved that all was well in the sleepy, beachside town. Tourist season was continuing without a hitch now that Frederick Critsworth's killers were safely behind bars.

At the bus terminal, she stood with Emma and Kacey while Grandma was seated on a bench, craning her neck to watch for the next bus to arrive. Larry, Gary, and Barry would soon be returning from their fishing trip.

"I can't thank you both enough for helping me," Kacey said. "I was so afraid my father would have to come back from his fishing trip to find me in jail."

"I knew it wasn't you," Emma said.

Sarah shot Emma a look.

Emma shrugged.

Sarah smiled, shaking her head. "It was no problem," she said. "I still feel bad for accusing you in the first place."

"It's okay," Kacey said. "I shouldn't have lied to you, Sarah. I'll never lie to you again." She gave Sarah a hug. "You are a great friend."

Sarah was speechless. When she opened her mouth to say something in response to Kacey, she heard Grandma yell, "Here they come!"

The bus approached, screeching to a halt. After a few passengers flooded out of the doors, they saw Larry's florescent Hawaiian shirt. Behind him was Gary, Kacey's father, and Barry, a man Sarah hadn't had a chance to meet yet. But she assumed it was him, since he was talking to both men.

"Lawrence," Grandma said, standing up to greet her husband.

Larry said, "Ruth, this is Barry."

"Oh, nice to meet you," Grandma said, shaking his hand.

Barry was muscular and reminded Sarah of Toby. She shuddered at the image of the man who had ended up being the man who'd strangled Critsworth—and to think, he'd had her in the back of his restaurant alone, with an abundance of potential weapons. She shook her head, dispelling the thoughts and returning her gaze to

Barry. His smile made its way to his eyes, and she could tell right away he was a genuinely nice person. Somehow, his demeanor put her at ease.

"And you must be Sarah," Barry was saying, smiling at Sarah. "I've heard so much about you."

"Hopefully all good things," Sarah said.

Barry laughed, then beamed at Emma. "And you must be Emma. I hear you make a really mean brownie," he said, wry look on his face. Sarah figured part of Larry had rubbed off on the man—he was a goof, just like her grandpa.

Emma seemed to have picked up on his sarcasm and put her hands on her hips. "I'll have you know that I can bake delicious chocolate chip cookies."

Sarah and Grandma snickered.

Emma shot them a look, shaking her head. "Traitors."

They all shared a laugh as they walked back to Grandma's light-pink Cadillac, placing Larry's things in the trunk—a red cooler on wheels and a small bag, among other things. Barry waved goodbye and headed off to his own car, his own cooler in tow. Sarah waved bye to Kacey and her father as they strode toward his vehicle, and she could hear Kacey say, "You'll never believe what happened to me, Dad..."

Sarah let out a sigh as she walked to the rear driver's side door. She opened it, and slid into the car.

Inside the vehicle, Grandma turned the key in the ignition, and the fin-tailed Cadillac coughed into life. They sat in silence for a moment as the car idled.

Grandma said, "Did you have a fun time, Lawrence?"

In the passenger seat, Larry was buckling his seat belt when he said, "Sure did. Caught some doozies. They're in the cooler in the trunk—I'll cook 'em up when we get home."

"Sounds good, dear," Grandma said, and backed out of the space, nearly running someone over in the process. "Oh, goodness," she muttered. "Don't want to join Toby and Flo, now do I..."

Larry gave a puzzled look.

"So, Grandpa," Sarah said, leaning forward as Grandma successfully maneuvered from the parking spot without hitting an innocent bystander. "What kind of fish did you catch?"

Larry turned, but was still obviously preoccupied by what his wife was talking about. He glanced back to Grandma. "What are you talking about?"

"The Critsworth thing that happened at Cecil's place. But don't worry, Lawrence, everything's fine with Cecil and his wife now."

"Yeah," Sarah chimed in. "They're doing well. I visited him yesterday and his Bed and Breakfast is open again. Already flooded with reservations, booked up for the rest of the summer, even into the fall."

"Good," Larry said. "So, what ended up happening?"

Grandma smiled. "Well, Sarah and Emma helped Adam catch the killers. Toby Keifer and Flo Gerkins."

"Flo? The waitress at the Banana Hammock?"

"That's the one."

"And Toby...he has the crab place, right?"

"Right."

A sudden realization struck Larry's face. "Oh yeah. The Crab Shack. I never go there. Read their food wasn't fresh. Good thing I always read the trusty paper to avoid places like that."

Sarah and Emma shot each other looks, and burst into a fit of laughter.

Larry glanced back at them, confused. "What?"

"Nothing," Sarah said, and she made another attempt to divert the conversation to lighter topics. "So, about the fish you caught..."

Larry's confused look transformed into one of great pride. "Oh, I caught the largest speckled trout I've ever seen. It's a gosh-darned beaut."

Sarah kept her grandpa focused on the topic of fishing and enjoyable activities as they made their way back to the apartment. There was another time and place to fill him in on all the nitty-gritty of the concluded murder investigation, but to her, now wasn't the time. Soon enough, this whole debacle would be something of the past, an episode that would be confined to town lore, having a place in the minds of the Cove's inhabitants, and eventually, a place in one of Grandma's scrapbooks.

CHAPTER 31

That night, everyone was excited to have an outing at Cascade Cove's amusement park at the southern end of the boardwalk. Sarah pulled her shoes on and noticed her cousin was spending more time in front of the mirror than usual, fiddling with her hair and makeup.

"Since when do you wear makeup?" Sarah asked.

"Since always," Emma said, adding the final coat of mascara and fluttering her eyelashes. She rummaged through her vanity drawers, looking for something. "Um, you haven't seen the eyelash curler, have you?"

Sarah grabbed her purse by the bed and started digging. "You mean this?" She held up the curler.

Emma turned to her. "Yeah, that's mine. Give it back." She put her hand out expectantly.

MEL MCCOY

"No way, Em. Not until you tell me why you're getting all dolled up." Sarah gazed into Emma's eyes. "Does this have anything to do with Mark?" Sarah said Mark's name in a sing-song tone, mocking Emma.

Emma said, "Give it to me!"

"No!"

Emma lunged out of her chair and landed on top of Sarah, grasping at the curler in her hand. "Sarah, stop! Give it back!"

Sarah smirked. "No way. Tell me first."

"I'll tell you nothing."

The door swung open and Grandma was standing there. "Girls!"

Sarah and Emma froze. It must have been quite a scene, with Sarah holding the curler up out of reach of Emma, who was on top of her.

"What is going on here?" Grandma asked, mouth agape.

"Sarah stole my curler and won't give it back," Emma said, getting off of Sarah and readjusting herself. She sat next to her cousin on the bed.

"Emma has a secret boyfriend, and she won't tell me who it is," Sarah said.

Grandma tapped her foot. "You are two grown women. Do I have to start treating you like children?"

Sarah and Emma both shook their heads in unison and quietly snickered.

"C'mon, girls, your grandpa is waiting. He is eager to order funnel cake. You know how he gets when he doesn't get his funnel cake."

Emma nodded. "I know," she said, and snatched the curler from Sarah's hand. She ran over to the mirror, curled the eyelashes of both eyes quickly, and spun around. "Okay, I'm ready."

Grandma eyed Emma.

Larry's voice carried down the hallway. "So, are we all about ready to go?" He peeked around the doorway and set his sights on Emma. "Emma," he said, gaze not wavering from her. "Why are you all made up?"

"Ha, I knew it!" Sarah shouted from the bed.

Emma rolled her eyes. "It's nothing. Can't a girl dress herself up anymore these days?"

Larry shook his head, confused. "All right, well, if we're all ready, then let's go!"

They made their way out the door, leaving Rugby, Winston, and Misty behind. Though, the pets didn't seem to mind. Sarah had Rugby and Winston out earlier chasing the Frisbee, and then later that day, to Adam's house chasing squirrels and rabbits. They'd gotten plenty of exercise, and it showed. Rugby was snoring away in a corner on his side, and Winston was on his stomach with his chin between his two front paws, looking up at them. Surely, he was waiting for them to leave so he could get some peace and quiet. And Misty was curled up on the back of the sofa, purring away.

They made their way out the door as Grandpa Larry yammered on and on about how he couldn't wait to get on the Ferris wheel and the merry-go-round. On their way there, Larry talked about how Faren's funnel cake was the best, and that he had to get an order of Camille's Caramel butterscotch apples. "They are the best!" he continued.

They walked through the entrance. Mark stood by the ticket booth ahead, waving at Emma.

Sarah saw him first and whispered to Emma, "Your boyfriend is looking for you."

Emma nudged her and turned to Grandma. "I'm going to go talk to Mark, Grandma."

"Okay," Grandma said. "Have fun. I'll be with your grandfather, making sure he doesn't give himself a tummy ache with all the sweets."

Emma smiled and gave Grandma a kiss on the cheek. "I have my cellphone in case you need me."

Grandma waved to her. "We won't. Go have fun!"

Larry fixed his gaze on Emma, who was running from them. Mark was grinning ear to ear and seemed to be glowing at the sight of Emma. "Where's she going?" Larry asked.

Grandma turned to Larry. "Mind your business, Larry." Then Grandma pointed to the funnel cake stand. "Look, there's Faren with the funnel cakes. Say, why don't we all go over there and get some?"

Grandma sure knew how to change the subject, Sarah thought and smiled. It was the happiest she'd been in a long time. It was a blessing to have her grandparents and cousin with her on the most wonderful night of the year. Sarah inhaled the fresh, salty night air. It was surely a night to remember.

She joined her grandparents eating funnel cake and riding the Ferris wheel. She was seated with her grandmother on one side and her grandfather on the other, facing them, when their cabin stopped at the top of the wheel. Sarah could see far beyond Cascade Cove and all the lights of houses and streets and buildings for miles. Then, she felt Grandma grasp her arm.

"Are you okay, dear?" Grandma asked

Sarah smiled. "More than okay," Sarah said, her gaze trailing as far as her eyes could see. An exhilarating breeze swept through Sarah's hair, and she closed her eyes, taking in the sweet scent that it carried. This was the life. This was exactly where she wanted to be. Where she needed to be. All her fears, anxieties, and problems drifted far, far away. There was another gust of wind that took Sarah's breath away momentarily, but she loved it.

The cabin rocked lightly from the wind, and Grandma tightened her grip on Sarah's arm. Larry interrupted her thoughts. "Ruth, darling, are you okay?"

"Yeah, it's just a little windy up here."

Sarah rubbed her grandma's hands, which were still clutching her arm. "It's okay, Grandma. Everything is going to be all right. Just focus on the beautiful scenery around you."

Grandma peered around. "I can see the boutique from here," she said, loosening her grip from Sarah's arm. "Oh, and there is the lighthouse."

The Ferris wheel started again, and they made their way back down. After the ride stopped, a gentleman helped them unhook the door and get off.

"I'll never get tired of the Ferris wheel. It's so much fun," Larry said.

Grandma gave him a look. "I don't know. I think I like being on the ground."

"But the sights are breathtaking."

Sarah nodded in agreement with her grandpa.

"So is the moon," Grandma said, "but you don't see me hopping on a rocket ship."

Sarah wore an amused smile as she glanced down,

watching her step. When she looked up again, she almost ran right into Adam.

"Enjoy the Ferris wheel?" Adam asked.

"Why, yes, it's beautiful up there," Larry said. "You should go with Sarah."

Adam shook his head. "I think I agree with Grandma on that. I'd rather be on the ground."

"Suit yourself," Larry said, "but you are missing out."

Everyone was quiet for a moment, until Grandma broke the silence. "Well, Larry, I think I'm beat. Let's say we call it a night."

Larry gave her confused look. Then he raised his eyebrows in realization. "Oh, of course," he said, with a grin. "I'll take you home." Over his shoulder, he winked at Sarah.

Sarah shook her head, and Larry and her grand-mother weaved their way through the crowds and into the night.

"So," Adam said. "You want to go on a ride or something?"

"No," Sarah said. "I think I'm about done here at the amusement park myself. Don't want too much of a good thing."

Adam bowed his head. "Oh," he said, scraping the toe of his shoe into the ground.

"But it's still early," Sarah said. "Why don't we go somewhere for a drink?"

Adam locked eyes with Sarah. "Yeah, I'm up for a drink."

"Great." Sarah took Adam's hand. "C'mon, follow me. I know just the place."

CHAPTER 32

After leaving the amusement park, Sarah led Adam down the boardwalk, toward Teek's. Of course, the outside facade would trick everyone who hadn't been to the surfer dude's newest bar, and Sarah could tell by Adam's confused look that he hadn't been there yet.

Adam studied the storefront, and shot Sarah a look. "Doing some late-night book shopping?"

"You'll see."

They strode through the door and into the poorly lit room. The man in the twenties-style suit sat at the table, curtains swaying behind him.

Adam whispered to Sarah, "What is this place?"

Sarah hushed him. "Just follow my lead," she said,

and pulled Adam to the table where the man sat, waiting. "We are here for a drink."

"Oh," the man said with a wink. "You are here for *that*." He pulled out an enormous, leather-bound book. "First, you must sign this. Don't worry," he said, voice now hushed, "we won't show the authorities."

Adam trained his eyes on Sarah, waiting for her to respond but when she didn't, he directed his gaze to the man. "I'm a cop," Adam said in a stern voice.

The man quickly closed the book, placing it back under the counter.

Sarah eyed Adam, giving him a swat on the shoulder.

The man got up and turned toward the curtain.

"You're so bad," Sarah whispered to Adam, as the man pulled the curtain back, exposing the hidden door.

Adam ignored Sarah. She could tell he was really confused and somewhat irate from his demeanor. He pushed past the man, opening the door only to be greeted by chatter, clinking glasses, and other sounds of the bar room. He glanced back at Sarah, looking slightly relieved.

Sarah couldn't help but laugh. She mouthed, "Sorry," to the man who had pulled back the curtain, but he waved her words away. She joined Adam in the doorway, and they both walked in together.

Teek caught sight of them, and his eyes grew with

excitement. "Sarah! Adam! Over here!" he shouted, waving them over.

Adam raised an eyebrow at Sarah. "Really? You brought me to Teek's bar?"

"He's a friend and I think you two need to make amends for whatever it is that happened between you."

Adam shook his head, but continued walking alongside Sarah to the bar.

Sarah hopped up on one of the stools and Adam joined her. Adam gave a less than enthusiastic "hey" to Teek, barely looking at him.

Teek was ecstatic. "Dude, I can't believe you're here." He gave Adam a strong pat on the shoulder that made Adam sway a bit. "What can I get you? I got lagers and some beers on tap. I also have mixed drinks I've invented myself. Anything you want, dude. This one will be on the house—for an old friend."

"Just whatever you have on tap will be sufficient," Adam said, his voice melding into the surrounding murmur.

Teek's gaze shifted to Sarah, his face still beaming. "I'll have my usual," Sarah said. "And gentle on—"

"The rum. No worries, dudette, I got you!" He scurried off to the other end of the bar for the ice, most likely preparing her drink first before pouring Adam's beer, so he could serve them at the same time.

Adam turned to Sarah. "'I'll have my usual?' How many times have you been here?"

Sarah's lips curled up. "A few."

Adam put his head in his hands, and moments later, Teek came back with their drinks.

"So, dude," Teek said to Adam, "what have you been up to? Putting a lot of baddies in the slammer?"

"I guess you can say that." Adam took a sip of his beer and grimaced, almost spitting it out. "What is this?"

"It's what we have on tap." Teek viewed the label on the nearby tap and tried pronouncing it but was unsuccessful.

"Never mind," Adam said. "I'm sorry, but this is terrible. Can I have something else?"

"Of course, dude," Teek said with a chuckle. "No one really likes the beer on tap anyway."

Adam gave Teek a look Sarah had never seen before. It was a surprised look, mixed with skepticism and worry.

Sarah had a couple sips of her mojito. She covered her mouth, trying to stifle a laugh, and instead let out a snort. This only made her laugh harder.

Adam looked at Sarah and began to laugh too. Teek glanced back and forth between them both and chuckled, unsure of what exactly they were laughing at.

Finally, Sarah spoke up, "Why don't you make him your latest? The Sandy Beach one."

"Ah," Teek said, nodding. "The Sandy Wave Margarita."

Adam shook his head. "I don't drink margaritas."

"This is not your average margarita," Sarah said.

"Yeah, I created it myself, and it's a huge hit with everyone," Teek said.

Sarah nudged Adam. "C'mon, try it. Or are you scared?"

Adam scoffed at her. "Of course, I'm not scared. I just don't drink margaritas, but if it's that important to you, then I'll give it a try."

"That's the spirit," Teek said, with excitement. "I'll be right back with your drink."

In a few moments, Teek came back with a huge margarita glass with a light peach, almost sand-colored concoction, topped with two umbrellas and an orange wedge.

Adam stared down at the drink. "This is massive. I'll never be able to finish all of this."

Teek smiled with pride. "Not many do," he said. "And the ones that do, often need to be wheeled out by a friend."

Adam dismissed his last statement. "I think I can

handle a margarita." He took a sip and his eyes went wide. "Woah!" How much alcohol is in this?"

Teek and Sarah shared a laugh.

After another sip, Adam said, "So, how'd you two meet, anyway? I remember you guys dated that one summer after our junior year."

Teek and Sarah exchanged a puzzled glance.

"What?" Adam asked.

"No way, dude. We didn't date," Teek said.

Confusion rippled across Adam's brow. "You both met at the bash on the beach, didn't you?"

"Yeah, but I would never date Sarah. She's like a kid sister to me, and besides, I thought something was going on between you two. I only helped her that night because you were a dud, dude. You never showed up."

Sarah nodded. "It's true. You told me to meet you at the Sand Dune hideout right outside the bash at nine p.m. I waited until after midnight."

Adam shook his head. "I only did that because I saw you with Teek. I saw you with him at the hideout, and he was leaning in to kiss you."

Sarah and Teek both looked at each other. Then it dawned on Sarah and her eyes went wide. "Oh, no. You got that all wrong. That night, I was dancing with Felicity. I had just met her that night and I fell, cutting my chin on a shell."

Teek chuckled. "That's right. You were bleeding like crazy. And you thought you might need stitches." To Adam, he said, "I took her over to the hideout where I had a first aid kit. We surfers need it often, and so we stash it behind one of the pillars. I was fixing up her chin."

"That was right before nine p.m.," Sarah said. "You must have seen him patching up my chin and thought he was kissing me."

"Oh my." Adam put his head in his hands.

"I thought you didn't like me or something," Sarah said, "and so I hung out with Teek and his friends for the summer. They tried to teach me how to surf."

Teek pursed his lips. "She wasn't very good."

"Hey," Sarah said with mock exasperation. "I got the hang of the boogie board."

Adam hung his head a moment, then said, "I'm sorry, Sarah. I didn't mean to stand you up. I was stupid back then."

"No worries," Sarah said with a smile. "Water under the bridge. I still had fun that summer. I only wished you were there."

"Could you imagine Adam surfing?" Teek said.

They all burst into laughter.

Sarah excused herself to go to the restroom. When she came out, she stopped and watched Teek and Adam talking. They were like long-lost buddies having a fantastic time. Adam was laughing so hard, she thought he might wet himself. She approached them, hopping back on her stool.

"Ah, Sarah's back," Adam said. "Teek was just telling me about that wave you missed."

"Yeah, she flipped completely upside down," Teek said. They both started laughing again.

Sarah shook her head. "Ha, ha, ha, laugh it up. We'll see who's doing somersaults in the water when we get you out there."

Adam chuckled. "No way I'm going out there."

"C'mon, dude," Teek said. "I can teach you."

Adam's phone blared. His face morphed from cheerful to serious. Sarah noticed the transformation and it gave her goosebumps. Quickly going from relaxed partygoer to pensive "superhero," Adam picked up his phone and his voice boomed: "I'll be right there."

Sarah and Teek waited as Adam got off his phone. "Sorry to cut this short, but I've got to go," he said, voice still stern.

"What's going on?" Sarah asked.

"Something at the amusement park," Adam said, getting up off his stool, leaving his margarita unfinished.

"What happened?"

Adam turned to face her, somber expression consuming all of his features. "Someone died."

Before Sarah could ask another question, Adam hurried out of the bar, going back to the amusement park, where they'd just been. Her heart raced and she wondered what had happened. Normally, she'd assume it was some sort of accident, but Cascade Cove was somehow different after the last two "incidents."

Teek stood nearby, slack-jawed. "Do you think it's another murder?" he asked, his voice the most serious Sarah had ever heard.

"I don't know. I hope it's just an accident."

She took a deep breath, knowing that it probably *was* just an accident.

But what if it wasn't?

"I hope you're right," Teek said, his voice barely audible among the growing murmur and the jukebox that was playing "Sweet Home Alabama" for the umpteenth time.

"Me too," Sarah said. She took one last sip of her mojito and set her glass down on the bar top. "Me too."

# # #

Thank you for reading! Want to help out?

Reviews are a big help for independent authors like me, so if you liked my book, **please consider leaving a review today**.

Thank you!

-Mel McCoy

ABOUT THE AUTHOR

Mel McCoy has had a lifelong love of mysteries of all kinds. Reading everything from Nancy Drew to the Miss Marple series and obsessed with shows like *Murder, She Wrote,* her love of the genre has never wavered.

Now she is hoping to spread her love of mysteries through her new Whodunit Pet Cozy Mystery Series. Centered around a cozy beachside town, the series features a cast of interesting characters and their pets, along with antiques, crafts such as knitting, and plenty of culinary delights.

Mel lives with her two dogs, a rambunctious and bossy Yorkie named Peanut, and a dopey, lazy hound (who snores a lot!) named Murph.

For more info on Mel McCoy's cozy mystery series, please visit: www.melmccoybooks.com

Connect with Mel:

Facebook: facebook.com/CozyMysteryMel
Twitter: twitter.com/CozyMysteryMel

WANT A FREE STORY?

Grab your free copy of *The Case of the Ominous Corgi*, a short cozy mystery featuring Rugby, Winston, and Misty. Simply visit www.melmccoybooks.com and click the "Free Story" link.

Made in the USA
Middletown, DE
30 November 2021